# A Sweetless Love

A Trilogy: Anişoara, Rozica, and the
Return of Prodigal Sons

David Kimel

# Dedication

To my children, Anca and Marius Kimel, whose love, encouragement and support is so much appreciated and valued.

# Contents


Dedication .......................................................................iii

Contents...........................................................................v

Foreword ........................................................................vii

About the Novel ..............................................................xvi

Acknowledgment .............................................................xviii

Anişoara ......................................................................... 1

Rozica ........................................................................... 95

The Return of the Prodigal Sons ............................... 191

About The Author ......................................................... 287

# Foreword

"A Sweetless Love" novel by David Kimel, presents the destinies of young people pursued by the communist repression apparatus, offering an overview of its surveillance and control mechanisms. The novel's action takes place in the city of Bucharest, Romania. Through the methodical reconstruction of the life of the main character, Daniel Cristescu—a young graduate at the beginning of his career who has repeatedly suffered from unjust accusations—the author highlights an era on which the history can influence an individual's destiny.

In the first story, Anişoara, the protagonist meets his new office colleagues, engineer Decu Alexandru, accountant Niculae Vintilă, and the young secretary, Anişoara Murguleanu. Beyond their office, in the workshop, Daniel meets the supervisor Stoica, the lathe operator Ion Decu and the comrade Cocoi, the Party Secretary. The young man felt warmly welcomed by his colleagues who help him understand his work tasks from the very first day. Warmly received, "Dan felt a sense of relief, stepping into this office where everything seemed new and fresh, with kind people offering him help to adapt to the requirements. It was his first job after graduating, and he felt lucky to be assigned to this newly established plant, equipped with new machinery brought from the Soviet Union" Another character soon appears in the office, Costin Faibiş, who worked at the plant's carpentry workshop. He was a childhood friend, neighbor and very much in love with Anişoara, the secretary, who only considered him as a brother.

From the very first day, engineer Decu Alexandru modified the norms calculated by Dan, who "looked on in surprise, bewildered that what was happening was illegal and contradicted what he had learned in school" The young man noticed that "some workers on the list had their salaries substantially increased with just a simple stroke of ink. Among them, the largest increase was given to Ion Decu, the brother of Engineer Alexandru Decu, the head of the department" With this discovery, the young new technician would be engaged in an endless conflict with the engineer and the plant workers whose earnings shrinked. On this fight, Anişoara, the secretary, would also get involved.

Daniel experiences a beautiful, shared love story with Anişoara, that "young, blonde, and very pretty girl [...] with large, curious blue eyes", who was "twenty-two years old." She confessed to him: "I have never loved anyone... until you" After their first meeting, he gives her a symbolic gift—a small cross, a sign of Christian faith and divine protection, telling: "This cross symbolizes my faith... in you. By keeping the cross, you are keeping me. Moreover, it is our connection to the Holy Lord". Touched, Anişoara promises never to part with her cross.

Once she becomes aware of the irregularities in the payroll records, she bravely confronted engineer Decu, arguing: "Every worker in the workshop receives 30–60 percent more than the base salary. None of the others get a single extra penny, except for those working on a quota. I think there is a limit to this too" and threatened to report the fraud to the Party and to Scânteia (the communist party newspaper). Supporting Daniel's claims, Mrs. Fazekaş, the Salaries Department Manager, holds engineer Decu accountable for the fraud, concluding: "What I cannot accept is favoritism. We do not change the norms just to brag about top workers, without considering the tens of thousands of lei in losses caused by inflating salaries". Mrs. Fazekaş reinstated Dan to his position as a norm accountant.

Anişoara becomes the victim of a plot orchestrated by Cocoi, the milling machine operator, and Decu, the lathe operator, both of whom raped and severely beat her to death, hoping the blame would fall on Daniel. Treated by Dr. Herşcovici, the girl manages to survive, though gravely injured, and deeply traumatized, after discharged from the hospital, Anişoara rejects Dan, feeling unworthy of his love: "I will never have children and will never kiss them. Don't you understand? My mouth has been defiled! My body has been defiled. The soul within me is defiled. I don't want to defile you too! You are free now. Find yourself a pure girl, as pure as you are. I do not deserve you anymore!". After he leaves, Anişoara takes a small bottle of poison she had, and drinks it. Her death coincides with Faibiş's arrest for killing Ion Decu, the lathe operator.

The second story, Rozica, starts with Anişoara's funeral service. Dan wandered along the banks of the Dâmbovița River. Near the sluice gate, he entered a restaurant where a group of workers from the nearby metallurgical plant got together for a drink. An idea occurred to him—to transfer to a new job closer to home, not only to shorten his commute but also to avoid the office where he had worked with Anişoara. He scheduled a meeting at the Metallurgical Plants with comrade Roşca, the party secretary, who advised him to formally request a transfer from his old job. Once again, Mrs. Fazekaş supported him recommending an old friend, Engineer Istrate, at the new workplace.

There, he met his new office colleagues: Engineer Istrate, "a woman over forty, blonde with blue eyes and an imposing stature, always dressed in very elegant tailored suits, maintaining a cautious distance from the rest of the team, which gave her an air of authority"; Mrs. Mănoiu, "the opposite in every way to her colleague—brunette, younger, very lively, and particularly competitive with her boss when it came to elegance. Both were married with no children, had husbands in high political positions"; and Bărbulescu, "a former career officer with a law degree, a gentle appearance and not a party member". Facing Daniel was Sorin Petrescu, a deaf-mute. Then there was Nestorescu, a former security officer dismissed from the Ministry of Internal Affairs for not meeting the "level of harshness required for the position".

Just like at his previous job, Dan demonstrated his skill and intelligence. "Even though he was new here, Dan noticed how the factory's products were deliberately damaged through so-called material-saving innovations, for which the authors were rewarded with a 15% salary bonus based on the calculated savings." Dan also displayed a practical mindset by proposing solutions, which led him accompany Engineer Crina Istrate to the minister's officials to present the Plant findings.

On their way back, Engineer Istrate invited Dan to various places, and she attempted to seduce him, saying that her husband is away for few days. Dan allowed himself to her seduction and gradually became aware of his lack of general knowledge compared to the people Crina socialized with. He decided to close this "gap" through reading. Regarding this project, Bărbulescu recommended the reading room of the Russian library. At one concert with Crina during intermission, he saw in the lobby Rozica Șfarț, a designer from the tooling department, and exchanged with her some words.

After the work, one day on the tram, the young man meets Rozica again. Upon learning Dan's destination, she also goes to the library and sits down right in front of him. At the end of the session, Dan walks Rozica home. She told Dan that her husband was imprisoned in Târgu-Mureş for fifteen years, that she had wanted to become a concert pianist, but "Fate had other plans." She gives him a brief account of her family's history: "We were Jews. The Germans came, the war started, my father was a liberal journalist and refused to perform forced labor. They caught him, arrested him, and nothing was ever heard of him since. My mother, an artist with a splendid voice, was no longer allowed to perform on stage. We survived with the help of family and friends. Three years ago, she fell ill with cancer and died. She wanted to see me settle down, so she arranged my marriage. My husband was an enthusiastic Zionist who organized illegal departures to Palestine, or Israel as it's called now, and he's rotting in prison."

A romantic relationship starts to develop between the two young people. Dan's two female colleagues, Mănoiu and Crina Istrate, quickly change their attitude toward him, following Dan refusal to continue his relationship with Crina. Rozica was interrogated by the Personnel Office and asked to give a statement "about her past and present connections. Nestorescu invites Dan, Sorin, and Bărbulescu to the restaurant near the factory and asks Dan if he has any enemies. He then warns him: "You're under investigation. Someone wants to bury you — they are saying you tried to kill a girl after raping her last summer. They say that's why you came to the factory, to cover your tracks."

From the discussion at the table, Dan concludes that "the two women in his group have teamed up to plot against him. Because he rejected their advances, they've decided to take revenge with the help of their husbands' wide authorities, even though they blatantly cheated on them."

As an instrument of the Romanian Communist Party, which conducted its directives, the Securitate played a key role in imposing a unified ideological orientation across society. To achieve this, many members of the Securitate resorted to actions that exceeded legal and constitutional norms, and in certain cases, to crimes and violations of human rights. Aware of these practices, Dan assesses his situation with clarity and feels "like prey surrounded by wolves." Even though he is innocent, no one would dare to stand up to the army of security officers tasked with punishing him: "The idea that the world around him is fair now collapses like a sandcastle. All that remains is a dense cloud of dust through which even the sun cannot shine."

Older people who lived through those early years of communism can easily recognize the portrait of Romanian society objectively depicted by David Kimel in the pages of this book. It is known that in the early years after coming to power, the regime led by Gheorghe Gheorghiu-Dej launched a large-scale offensive against the structures of the old society. Terror was imposed on all levels of Romanian society: religious persecution, the elimination of political opponents, the dissolution of political parties and civil society structures — all well known to Dan, who reflects: "The fates of individuals depend so much on the power of others that truth, justice, and fairness become meaningless and are transformed into tools of oppression against the innocent. Those who should have been the true judges become the victims of the criminals who wield unlimited power over those ruled. He knows that once that infernal machine of the Securitate is set in motion, nothing can stop it. Without intending to, he has put Rozica in danger — just as he had with Anișoara not long ago — and this thought causes him pain: "For the second time, those seeking revenge on him are striking at innocent people connected to him. He could see how his presence in the lives of those close to him was harmful, and he could not forgive himself for it."

The final episode follows Dan and Rozica as they attempt to escape to Israel, driven by the hope of finding salvation in the Holy Land. Rozica disguises herself as a boy, and the two travel cautiously by train. On the train to Sibiu, they encounter Father Ștefan Suțu, a suspicious priest who questions Rozica and notices her knife, which bears the crest of his noble family. Ștefan confesses to Rozica that he deeply loved her mother, Simha, but their parents forbode such a relationship. Heartbroken, he became a monk, but seeing Rozica's resemblance of her mother, his old obsession reignited. He offers the couple shelter but secretly betrays Dan by notifying the secret police (Securitate) that Dan is a wanted criminal planning to flee the country.

Dan narrowly escapes arrest, hiding in a chapel. Thinking that the police know his appearance, he tries to disguise himself. Meanwhile, Rozica realizes Ștefan's obsession with her. When he tried to assault her, Rozica stabbed him in self-defense. Dan, arriving at the scene just then, Rozica, in a state of panic not recognizing him, stabbed him as well. Surviving, the authorities arrested the couple and the priest, charged the young people with treason, and attempted illegal escape. Rozica and Dan received harsh prison sentences, while Father Ștefan was defrocked and received jail time for rape.

The novel closes on a bittersweet note, while Rozica and Dan eventually were allowed to exchange censored letters in prison, finding solace in the hope that they might one day be free.

"A Sweetless Love" by David Kimel, is a gripping story of survival, betrayal, and hope set against the oppressive backdrop of early communist Romania. Kimel's story is a powerful testimony to the harsh realities of early communist Romania, exploring themes of love, betrayal, resilience, and the human spirit's capacity to endure even in the darkest times.

**Doina Bălțat**

# About the Novel

David Kimel's new creation, "A Sweetless Love," reaffirms his distinctive narrative style at an elevated level of mastery. True to his style, the author creates an atmosphere full of realism, where the characters are confronted with life sequence emotional moments marked by both their normality and, at times, their abnormality. The actions of the main characters often force them to make decisions that do not always align with the plans they had carefully crafted.

With remarkable attention to detail, David Kimel constructs situations where distinctly human feelings—love, compassion, suffering, hope, despair, trust, and mistrust—collide, with the power to derail even the most intimate and longed-for plans. The love stories of the characters are deeply human, pure, and full of promises of happiness, creating the impression that the reader is directly involved in these experiences. The scenes depicting the action seem almost photographed or filmed, as the author presents each frame with a wealth of detail that imprints itself in the reader's memory, as if they were an active participant in this journey.

In this flow of character development, where the lives of the characters intersect throughout the novel, the author carefully emphasizes the moral purity, rationality, and survival instinct of the main character, Daniel Cristescu. The novel's plot is skillfully driven, with the abundance of details inviting reflection from all perspectives—artistic, social, familial, emotional, and historical— set in contrast to the morally weak or, more precisely, the reprehensible behavior of certain characters.

As the story unfolds, the reader becomes emotionally attached to the main characters—Anișoara, Rozica, and Daniel— following with emotion the situations they are forced to navigate.

Once again, author David Kimel delights us with a wonderful literary creation that ensures a pleasant, engaging, and well-documented reading experience.

Ionel Gurău

# Acknowledgment

It is said that gratitude is a virtue. I have many reasons to be grateful to a significant number of people who extended a helping hand in times of need, guiding me through moments of doubt, situations where every path seemed hopelessly blocked, or simply offering a much-needed word of encouragement. How could I not be grateful to the heavens, which, through the power of Divinity, have always guided me with protective angels embodied in family members, friends, and acquaintances with hearts of gold?

To my wife, Valeria, who has been my guiding light and life companion for the past 64 years and who has given me children whose love and devotion surpass any praise, I am deeply grateful for her understanding, trust in me, and the personal sacrifices imposed by life's circumstances. To her, I owe the peace and warmth of a home that has helped erase from memory the perennial hardships encountered beyond its walls.

Uprooted from the soil of the country that gave me life, I have strived to grow new roots in the welcoming land of Canada, where I knew no one and did not even speak the language of my new country. Yet, by the grace of Providence, I have achieved here what was not possible in my homeland—I have prospered and surrounded myself with family and friends. To all of them, I am profoundly grateful.

When time granted me the opportunity to pour my feelings onto fresh ink-stained pages, transforming thoughts into images easily understood by any reader, I was met with the goodwill of true friends who encouraged my attempts, selflessly guided me toward success, and smoothed the transition from a technical career to a literary one. Among them, Mr. and Mrs. Dumitru Puiu Popescu, editors of the Romanian-language magazine Observatorul in Toronto, were the first to publish my writings in their magazine. I owe it to them that, for nearly two decades, my articles have been regularly featured in the Subjective column.

Many other remarkable souls have supported me with encouragement, guidance, and advice, for which I remain deeply grateful, including writers Elena Buică, Veronica Pavel Lerner, the late Gavril Morariu, Daniela Cupșe Apostoaei, Codruț Miron, and Leonard Voicu, who founded the Mihai Eminescu Literary Circle in Montreal for Romanian writers. To them, I owe my respect and deepest thanks.

This book is now the collective product of individuals committed to bringing the works of lesser-known writers to life, taking on the risks of results that will only become clear over time. At Paramount Book Publishing, I had the pleasure of meeting people whose kindness, assistance, and guidance cannot go unnoticed: Joe Brandon, who had the patience and tact to dispel any uncertainty about entering an unfamiliar publishing process with institutions located hundreds of kilometers away; April Woods & Gary Miller, my Senior Project Managers and coordinator of this endeavor, whose warmth and dedication won me over; and the artist who designed the book cover, capturing the very essence of my novella—though I do not know his/her name, I remain indebted.

Respect and sincere gratitude to all the individuals mentioned above and to the entire team at Paramount Book Publishing for bringing this book to life.

David Kimel

# Anișoara

David Kimel

# Anişoara

It was early July in the year 1956 in Bucharest, Romania. On the corridor of the mechanical workshop, a side door with a frosted glass panel made Dan stop in his tracks for a moment. Nervously, he straightened his posture and cleared his throat. It was his first day of work in this place, and he had no idea who his new colleagues would be. He knocked on the door and pressed down on the handle.

He entered a large, bright room with four desks. The one in the corner by the window was unoccupied. Three other desks were lined up against the opposite wall, with two of them occupied. At the desk near the window, a young, blonde, and very pretty girl put down her pencil and looked at him with curious, wide, blue eyes. At the desk near the door, a man around 30 years old with thinning hair slicked back stood up.

"How can we help you?" the man asked.

"Good morning. My name is Daniel Cristescu. I'm a new employee and a work quota clerk. Are you Engineer Decu?"

"No. Engineer Decu's office is on the corner. I'm Niculae Vintilă, the accountant, and this comrade here is Anişoara Murguleanu, the secretary of Comrade Decu. Your desk is this one here," Comrade Vintilă said, shaking Dan's hand and guiding him to the middle desk.

Instead of another greeting, Dan smiled at the blue-eyed girl on his right as he surveyed the room and the wide desk with many drawers. On the wall in front of him, a large window revealed the interior of the mechanical workshop, where several lathes were aligned along the windows facing the inner courtyard. A row of machines for milling gear wheels stood behind the lathes, along with other machines serving different functions. Near the window in the workshop, a man with silver hair, only his nape visible, was sitting at a desk piled with papers. Dan would soon learn that this was the foreman, Comrade Stoica, the head of the workshop. Everything in the workshop gleamed and looked like a model showroom from an exhibition with new equipment and workers in overalls.

In the middle of Dan's desk was a stack of printed forms, handwritten notes, dimensioned sketches, and oil stains, all waiting to be dealt with. Seeing Dan still standing behind his desk, trying to decipher the notes on one of the papers atop the stack, Comrade Vintilă addressed him:

"Those are the technological sheets from last week, normed by Comrade Decu. You'll have to prepare the payroll report for each worker by adding up the hours normed on those sheets. Comrade Murguleanu can show you how to complete these lists. She's been handling this until now."

Dan thanked him while the young woman told him that in the middle drawer, he would find a notebook with the necessary information compiled by her over the past few weeks. She thought it would make it much easier for Dan to get his bearings by following her example. Dan opened the drawer and indeed found a notebook with hand-drawn lines containing information about the workers, their qualifications, and their hourly wages. He thanked her, smiling. She responded from behind her desk with a slight nod of her head.

Dan felt a warm sense of relief as he settled into this office, where everything seemed new and fresh, with friendly people offering help to ease his transition. This was his first job after finishing school, and he felt fortunate to have been assigned to this plant, which had just opened and was equipped with new machinery brought from the Soviet Union. In the middle drawer, Dan also found a stack of timecards, which he placed on the wide surface of the desk. Following the previous lists made by Comrade Murguleanu, he lined new pages in duplicate, using carbon paper, in the unused sections of the notebook he had found. In an adjacent notebook, he began to record, in separate columns, the hours accumulated by each worker, copying the norms written in red pencil by Comrade Decu on each work order.

At some point, the quiet was interrupted by the appearance of a young man with blonde hair, wearing a checkered sports shirt and holding a folder.

"Hello! Have you heard the latest news? I think it was even announced over the loudspeaker."

"No, I haven't turned it on yet," said Comrade Murguleanu, standing up to switch on the radio. "What's it about?"

"On Sunday, the swimming pool by the lake opens. Everything is almost ready, and now they've brought the cinders for the volleyball court. Comrade Roman said we should get our swimsuits ready. He mentioned there will be boats, too."

"I don't believe it," said Comrade Murguleanu. "On Sunday, we, the UTM (The Young Workers Union) committee members, have to go to the district office. Who's going to oversee the opening if we can't be there? Let me introduce you to Comrade…"

"Daniel Cristescu," said Dan, standing up. "I'm new here. I started today."

"Faibiş, Costin. Welcome! I work at the carpentry workshop. You'll see it on the way to the lake. Good luck!" said the young man, shaking Dan's hand. "Do you live nearby?"

"No, across Grant Bridge. Do you live close?"

"Me and Anişoara, Comrade Murguleanu, live on the same street, here, behind the lake, in Băneasa."

"That's great; you have someone to talk to on your way

home."

"When it happens. She's always busy with initiatives and activities," Faibiș said, casting a sidelong glance at Anișoara.

"And what about you, taking advantage? Waiting for others to fight while you reap the rewards?" the girl retorted angrily.

"Come on, enough! We have work to do today!" Comrade Vintilă intervened.

Everyone returned to their desks while Faibiș, standing in the doorway, called out to the newcomer again:

"Good luck! Stop by sometime so we can talk more." Dan nodded slightly and returned to his tasks.

Before lunch, a tall, broad-shouldered man, neatly dressed in a suit and tie, entered the office and sat at the table in the corner, between the window and the workshop window. Glancing around, he noticed Dan.

"Are you the new norm accountant?"

"Yes, Comrade Decu. I've been assigned to your section."

"Did they explain what you need to do?"

"Yes, Comrade Vintilă and Comrade Murguleanu showed me."

"Before you take the list to Work and Wages, give it to me

to check."

"I think it's ready. I just need to calculate the totals," Dan said.

"All the better. May I look?" Dan picked up the notebook with lined sheets of paper from his desk and handed it to the supervisor. Comrade Decu took the list and began reviewing the hours and the total wages earned by each worker in the section while asking Dan:

"What did you say your name was?"

"I'm sorry I didn't introduce myself. My name is Daniel Cristescu. You can call me Dan."

"Alright, Dan. We need to make some changes here. The norms for certain items are incorrect. Can I have the technological sheets, please?" Dan went to his desk to retrieve the stack of standardized sheets.

Comrade Decu took out a fountain pen from his jacket pocket and began altering the norms, writing over the red pencil entries with new figures in ink. Dan watched, surprised and troubled, realizing that what was happening now was illegal and went against what he had learned in his training.

"Wouldn't it be better to time these operations?" the young man asked timidly.

"No. We don't have time for that now. Maybe another time..."

Dan returned to his desk, disheartened, forced to change many of the numbers he had previously calculated. Some workers' wages were significantly increased with just a simple stroke of ink. Among them, the highest increase was next to another name: Decu Ion, lathe operator, probably related to Comrade Engineer Decu Alexandru, the head of the department.

This situation seemed contradictory. Party policy condemned such abuses, which harmed the pace at which the working class was building socialism. It was his duty to expose these abuses. Maybe not today, on his first day. Perhaps there were other violations he didn't know about yet, or maybe more people were involved, of whom he was unaware. That's why it was better to wait and see how deep the mire went.

At lunch, Comrade Anișoara took two sandwiches wrapped in parchment paper from her purse.

"At the end of the corridor, on your way to the lockers, you'll find a café where you can buy something to eat if you don't have anything," she told him.

"No, thank you. I never eat at this time," Dan assured her. "I'd rather check the salary lists one more time before taking them to Work and Wages. Maybe you could take a look at them before I submit them."

"You know what? Now that we're colleagues, please just call me Anișoara, like everyone else. And no more formalities. Now, please, take this sandwich from me. No protests, please! No fuss!" Anișoara handed him one of the two neatly wrapped sandwiches.

"Really, you shouldn't have. Now what do I do? Thank you," Dan said, accepting the sandwich.

"So, how do you find it here on your first day?" she asked. He wanted to share more of his thoughts about what he had observed on this first day at work but realized it wasn't the right moment. So, he simply said:

"I'm pleased with everything I've seen. I was lucky to be assigned here."

"I felt the same way," Anișoara said. "There are many interesting comrades. I'll introduce you to them. Some fought in the underground. Take Comrade Decu, for example—he came from the USSR. He went to university there. He was even imprisoned before, back when he was a lathe operator at Grivița Roșie. (A railway depot where many strike workers were shot by gendarmes in 1933)."

Dan listened attentively to Anișoara's words. Then he asked:

"But I noticed there's another Comrade Decu. Was he also an underground fighter?" Anișoara leaned in and whispered to Dan:

"No, he's the brother of Comrade Engineer Decu. He's got a wife and kids, but he chases skirts. Tell me, what kind of Party member does that? He's an arrogant, sleazy man who disgusts me. But because they're brothers, I have no choice but to smile at him. He works at the lathe near the window. Don't turn your head, he's watching us, trying to get my attention."

Dan finally understood why Comrade Decu had asked for the salary lists.

"Tell me," Anişoara continued, "why are you a norm accountant and not a norm setter? Is there a difference?"

"After the army, I went to a technical school. In norm-setting, you must have more experience. I learned that the clearest way to fix a norm is when each operation is timed, especially in mass production. You select three people to perform the same operation, time them individually, and at the end, their average becomes the work standard for everyone."

"Is that why you suggested timing the operation to Comrade Decu?"

"Yes. I don't understand why the norm had to be revised." Anişoara scrutinized him with her clear azure eyes.

"Do you really not understand?" Dan remained silent.

After lunch, when everyone returned to work, Faibiş came

back into the office.

"How's it going?" he asked Dan. "Did you take the list to Wages?"

"Not yet. I want to check it once more, then I'll ask Comrade Anişoara to see if what I did is correct."

"Are you going to take him upstairs to introduce him to the comrades?" Faibiş asked the girl.

"Do you want to introduce him?"

"I can do it. No problem," Faibiş said.

Anişoara shrugged without saying anything. Dan handed her the complete lists on two or three pages. After a brief review, she handed them back.

"Take only the original pages. Leave the copies in the notebook so we can keep track of what we submitted."

Faibiş opened the door for him, and the two walked down the corridor, which was dimmer than the office. Along the way, Faibiş pointed out what was behind the doors they passed.

"Here's the materials and tools storage for the entire department. Comrade Manea, the storekeeper, has theater tickets for all performances, the cost of which is deducted from your salary. Here's the electrical workshop, where burnt-out motors are rewound. This is the café, and over there are the women's and men's lockers."

They entered the administrative area, where the offices lined on one side, and the corridor was lit brightly by the courtyard surrounding the central building. They climbed the stairs to the first floor. On this floor, the corridor, lined with offices on both sides, was discreetly lit by filtered neon lights placed at equal intervals, and the floor was covered with a plush brown carpet stretched from wall to wall. Faibiş took him into several offices, including Work and Wages, after which they made their way back down the white marble stairs toward the technical department.

"Let's have some coffee at the café," Faibiş suggested to Dan.

They sat at one of the tables, and a girl brought them two cups of coffee in thick, white-glazed porcelain mugs. Faibiş paid.

"You seem like a serious man, and I believe I can trust you." Dan nodded while Faibiş continued. "Let's start with Anişoara. She is a wonderful girl but too gullible. Because she is honest and pure, she thinks everyone is the same. She only sees angels around her. Don't laugh! That's the truth. I don't know how to convince her that the world is cruel, that people are selfish and will take advantage of her weakness. I can't always be there to protect her from these creatures. Do you understand what I'm saying?"

Dan, looking him in the eyes, nodded again without saying

a word.

"I care a lot about Anișoara. We grew up together, and she's like a sister to me. It's still the same, except here, since the factory opened, she's been surrounded by flatterers who praise her and burden her with all kinds of tasks. From the youth organization, the Party, the union—and she doesn't know how to say no. You'll be with her all day. Take care of her, act like a brother, because there are many hungry sharks who want to take her. Will you promise to do this for me?"

Dan smiled:

"I promise! It seems like you're head over heels in love with Anișoara. Come on, tell me, am I right?"

"I am! I always have been! God help anyone who dares lay even a finger on her!" Dan understood that the threat also applied to him.

The rest of the day passed without anything important, except for the fact that Anișoara took him to meet comrade Stoica, the workshop foreman, comrade Cocoi, the Party secretary, and comrade Dinescu, from the union. Back at comrade Stoica's office, Dan asked him what orders were scheduled for the next day. The foreman leafed through a few technical files on his desk, showing them to him.

"You know, I'd like to note the start and end times on each one. Do you think that's possible?" Dan asked. The foreman was silent for a moment before replying:

"I don't see why not."

"Then tomorrow morning, before you hand them out, I'll come by to write down the order number and the name of the person assigned to each. Do you agree?" The foreman indicated he had no objections.

Before the workday ended, the machines in the workshop were stopped, and the workers cleaned them of the metal shavings left from machining. During this time, Faibiş showed up, as expected:

"Are you coming home with me?" he asked Anișoara.

"I don't think so. Emilia asked me to go shopping with her. There are only a few days left until her wedding, and there's still a lot to buy. I promised to help her."

Emilia was another childhood friend of Anișoara's, who also worked in the administration department. In the office, everyone locked away their paperwork, ready to leave. Anișoara stayed behind to wait for Emilia.

As he left the factory, Dan headed toward the tram stop. His first day of work had come to an end. In these few hours, he felt as if he had stepped into a new, unexpectedly dynamic world full of impressions that needed careful filtering. He was glad to have met Anişoara, a charming girl, Faibiş, who was likable but jealous and suspicious, and the others, especially the foreman Stoica, who had made a good impression on him. He didn't know how to repay Anişoara's kindness for the sandwich she had given him at lunch, and he was embarrassed that he didn't have any money for the next day so as not to find himself in the same situation again.

He lived with his aunt, a widow from the war, who supported herself with what she earned by sewing for the neighbors as she was a seamstress. But with these hard times, when everyone was poor after the war, it wasn't much, especially now when there was hardly anything to be found, when the shop shelves were empty, and even with clothing coupons, there wasn't much to buy. It was enough that, thanks to her, he was able to finish school, that she washed and mended his clothes, and that she made sure he had food every day, which they shared. Maybe after receiving his first paycheck next week, he would be able to repay Anişoara's gesture in some way. However, the next day, at lunchtime, he would be the first to leave the office to avoid being in the same situation as today.

***

A few days had passed, and Dan's first week of work was almost over. It was Thursday, the payday. Over the last few days, he had started to feel that some of the workers weren't too pleased with his effort to record the time of the operations in the technical files. Some had even complained to comrade Stoica about it. The foreman responded that it was Dan's duty, so no one could change the new rule. The most offended seemed to be comrade Decu, who worked at the lathe near the partition window of the office. When Dan reached his lathe, comrade Decu greeted him with an ironic and slightly aggressive smile:

"I see you're good at spying on the workers!"

"I'm not spying on anyone. I'm just doing my duty, just like you're doing yours."

"What kind of duty is it to be on someone's back for every move they make?" the lathe operator asked.

"Why don't you ask the people who put me here?" Dan responded, turning his back on him. The man at the lathe threw the wrench he was holding after Dan, hitting the cement floor of the workshop. Dan turned back, frowning at the man.

"Sorry. It slipped out of my hand." Dan didn't say anything and walked away.

After the lunch break, he brought the payroll registers for the entire technical department and the money he was supposed to distribute to the employees, all in a small canvas bag. Before three o'clock, people he had never seen before started coming to him. They were scattered across various departments in the factory. Many of them knew each other, and as Dan searched for their names on the lists spread out on the office table, he asked them to sign for the money while he counted out the amounts listed on the payroll. When everyone had received their pay, Dan was surprised to find almost seven lei left at the bottom of the drawer.

"That's normal," comrade Vintilă assured him. "With a payroll fund of nearly fifty thousand, a few leftover coins are bound to happen."

Dan joked, "Well, lucky me! Tonight, I'll party hard. With musicians too!"

***

The following Monday, Dan collected the timecards from the electric clock board and then went to foreman Stoica to note which orders were coming into production. Anișoara entered the office, flushed and eager to talk. The day before, she had been celebrated as the maid of honor at Emilia's wedding. A splendid wedding, with tables set up on three sides in the middle of the courtyard and guests made up of the closest friends and neighbors from the street. Everyone partied until late, well past midnight.

Dan pulled out the ledger to calculate last week's wages and began lining new pages in duplicate, just as he had done before.

Faibiş continued to come into the office two or three times a day, whether he had any new information or not, but this time, he was in a bad mood, unusual for his typically cheerful character.

"What's new? Were you at Emilia's wedding last night?" Dan asked.

"He made a fool of himself," Anişoara interjected. "He drank too much and started picking fights with the guests."

"Not everyone can be as successful as you," Faibiş retorted. "She acted like a star over there. It was as if she was the bride! All smiles, dancing, and showing off. She turned me down twice…"

"That's because you were rude. Others invited me before you did," the girl responded.

"You were the one who was rude! A true friend doesn't act like that without respect. What do you think I am, huh? And so, what if we've known each other forever? Respect shouldn't disappear…" The girl fell silent. Faibiş threw one last glance behind him and left.

In the office, only the sound of a folk dance, occasionally pierced by shouts, could be heard blasting from the wall-mounted radio. Everyone was focused on their work when engineer Decu appeared. After leafing through a few papers on his desk, comrade Decu asked Dan if he had finished the payroll report.

"It's ready, comrade engineer," Dan said, standing up to

hand the list to his boss. He examined the figures for each employee again and then asked for the technical files. Dan handed them over. While the engineer was adjusting the work quotas in front of Dan, who stood watching everything, he addressed his superior:

"I don't think it's possible to change the norm for this task."

The engineer looked up, surprised.

"Why not?"

"Because that operation was completed in almost half the allocated time."

"How do you know that?"

"Because I was there."

"I don't believe you. I know better. Now, get back to your place!" the engineer said.

"Comrade engineer, I'm not lying. I have the record of every task completed last week here. I can tell you the time taken for each operation."

"Are you trying to teach me how to set quotas? Mind your own business if you want to keep working in this department! I'm the only one who is deciding here, and no one else. Remember that!"

"As you wish," Dan replied, returning to his desk. "But with all due respect, I'm not changing any of the quotas in my payroll list!"

The engineer screwed the cap back onto his fountain pen and left the office. Anişoara widened her eyes as if she were seeing Dan for the first time. Comrade Vintilă shook his head doubtfully and said without looking at Dan:

"I don't think this will end well. There will be consequences."

Dan felt that he couldn't control the nervous tremors that had overtaken him. When the engineer returned, he handed Dan back the technical files and the payroll list without a word. After the lunch break, Dan submitted them to the Payroll Department.

***

In the following days, except for foreman Stoica, very few of the workers in the section responded to Dan's greetings. During each round through the workshop, with his papers clipped onto a thick cardboard folder, most of them pretended not to notice his presence, and some even positioned themselves in his way, preventing him from observing the progress of the operations.

By midweek, the sun shone gloriously over a clear, uniform sky, stretched like a bluish canvas across the horizon. Faibiş entered the office, sweating.

"Hey there, buddy. Have you already taken a dip at the

pool?" Dan asked, laughing when he saw his shirt sticking to his damp skin.

"Hell no. I should've gone there instead of coming here. Today's race day. Are you coming with me to the racetrack?" Faibiş asked Dan.

"I'd rather go to the lake than the racetrack," the young man replied.

"Suit yourself. What about you?" he asked Anişoara.

"The lake is more appealing. I even brought my swimsuit from home."

Faibiş shrugged and left.

After work, Dan and Anişoara went together to the newly opened lakeside. It was indeed beautiful, with new buildings for changing rooms, showers, sports fields, and even a club in the style of a Swiss chalet. It had a bar, sandwiches, and chic tables on the terrace overlooking the beach. Anişoara came out of the changing room in a black one-piece swimsuit, while Dan wore swimming trunks his aunt had sewn from a towel with stripes of various colors arranged horizontally. They each took a towel from a bench and lay down in the sun on the golden sandy beach, bathed by the waters of the lake. Stretched out on their stomachs, side by side, she closed her eyes in the sunlight while he gazed at her strands of hair swaying in the wind, glistening translucent like a flame of gold. This girl was truly beautiful, he thought. Her face, body, mind, and soul came together perfectly in a kind of rare and unique harmony. Faibiş had every reason to be jealous. A short distance away from them, a woman with sunburned skin and thick, abundant black hair sprouting from all sides of her swimsuit, even under her arms, sat smoking on the bare sand.

After a while, Anişoara stood up to look at the lake, which widened and became more crowded toward the city side, where there were boats, restaurants, and public pools. On the opposite side of the beach, there was an island at a distance equivalent to two or three lengths of a swimming pool. Dan was still lying on his stomach when Anişoara touched his shoulder, saying:

"I'm going to swim to the island. Are you coming with me?"

Dan got up to gauge the distance.

"Isn't it a bit too far?"

"I don't know. If it's too far, I'll turn back."

Dan hesitated.

"Why? It's so nice here..."

"Come on!" she said, standing up.

Dan watched her enter the water and followed her. He had never swum such a long distance before. Without looking back, she glided easily through the warm summer water, two or three steps ahead of him. He tried to pace himself, afraid of using up all his energy before he was sure he could reach the opposite shore. But on this side, the bank was steep and slippery, covered in bushes and green vines that weren't very welcoming. Anişoara searched for a spot where it was easier to climb up, and Dan, grabbing a branch, extended his hand to help her. They sat down next to each other on the shore, breathing deeply and quickly. Anişoara found a small stick and started drawing circles, scratching the surface of the ground:

"Did you see that lady smoking next to me? I hate women who don't care about their appearance. At the electrical workshop, there's another woman just like her. She wears silk stockings, but her legs are covered with black hair from top to bottom. It's disgraceful. And she was the same. On top of that, she smoked…"

"I guess in the countryside, people don't really care about hairy legs. I don't recall my mother doing anything to get rid of it…" Dan said thoughtfully.

Anişoara looked at him and suddenly jumped up in horror:

"Ants! You're covered in ants!" Dan jumped up as well.

There were large, reddish ants crawling all over his swimming trunks and legs. She helped him brush them off but soon realized she was also covered in them too. She started to itch all over:

"I'm going in the water. Help me, please. Give me your hand!" Dan extended his hand, and she eased herself into the lake.

"Don't look at me. Turn around, please. I need to wash my swimsuit!"

Dan turned, and the girl moved a few steps away to hide behind a bush. Suddenly, she let out a terrified scream:

"Ah! There are fish here. Big fish around me. Give me your hand so I can get out! Don't look at me!"

Dan grabbed onto a branch and extended his hand. She slid through the water in front of him, a white mermaid with the body of Aphrodite, her breasts as firm as those sculpted in marble. Dan turned his back as Anișoara put on her swimsuit. They then swam back to the other side of the shore.

Once back on the beach, they stretched out again on their towels to dry in the sun. She said,

"I read somewhere that in the USSR, children are taught not to make a distinction between boys and girls. They say the human body is beautiful just the way it is, and there's nothing shameful about seeing someone of the opposite sex naked. Do you think that's true?"

"I don't know. Maybe if children are used to it from a young age, it might not matter. For example, if I were on a beach surrounded by nudists, I don't think I'd feel anything. But if I were in front of a single naked woman, I'm sure the result would be different."

"Even if you were in front of your mother or sister?" she asked.

"If I were in front of them, I'd run away. I'd gouge my eyes out like Oedipus!"

"But in front of me?" Anișoara watched him closely, not just his eyes but every gesture and movement. Dan, embarrassed, replied,

"With you, it's different... You're unreal. You're like ether, more of an idea than a woman. I see something sacred in you, like in an icon. I could never touch you..."

Anișoara turned her head, visibly moved. She stood up from the towel.

"Let's leave. Will you walk me home?"

"I'll walk you."

For a while, they walked in silence. Then, as they passed through the park on a path, she took his arm with both hands:

"And you're different too. I've only known you for a few days, but in your presence, I feel safe, protected, and calm. I think you're the only person I trust enough to open my soul to, to let my guard down. Do you understand?"

"I understand. But Faibiş? You know how much he loves you."

"Faibiş is different. I've known him since we were kids. He's like a brother to me. I care for him deeply, but his insecurity, his constant need for proof of affection, his jealousy, and the way he turns to drink when things don't go his way all unsettle me. No, he's not like you. Right now, he's off-betting on horse races, trying to impress me with the money he wins. No question, Faibiş is not for me!"

They stopped at a bench in front of a restaurant with a wide terrace.

"It's gotten cooler. Put your arm around my shoulders," Anişoara requested. Dan pulled her close to his chest. She rested her head on his shoulder. They sat like that for a while, daydreaming with open eyes. Then she suddenly started:

"Do you have someone special in your life?"

"No. I don't have anyone. I've met a few girls, but I wasn't really drawn to any of them. I don't know how to explain it. With a pair of nylon stockings, most of them would be easy to win over. But I have neither the money nor the time for that kind of thing."

"Then why… why don't you kiss me?"

"Because of Faibiş. I promised him I'd be like a brother to you. Before I kiss you, I need to tell him I love you and…" Anişoara jumped off the bench as if she had been burned:

"You need his permission to kiss me?"

"No! You don't understand. It's a matter of honor. I gave my word. I need to take it back first."

She sat back down on the bench.

"I'm twenty-two years old. Most of my friends are married, and some even have children. My parents keep asking me, 'What are you doing? Do you want to become an old maid?' I've never loved anyone… until you. Do you believe me?"

Dan hugged her with both arms, pulling her close to his chest and whispering in her ear:

"I believe you, my dear. I believe you like I've never believed anyone before. And I love you just as much."

It had grown dark. They walked, Dan's arm wrapped around her shoulders, until they reached the house where Anişoara lived. They stopped Dan leaning against the wall by the street. She pressed herself against him, feeling safe and happy yet filled with a terrible sadness that they had to part. She glanced left, then right down the street, and finally, she threw her arms around his neck in a tight embrace, sealed with a kiss on the lips, before running into the courtyard.

***

The next morning, all signs pointed to another splendid summer day with a clear sky and a scorching sun. Dan woke up with an inner sense of joy and optimism, unlike anything he had ever experienced. A surge of vigor and a love for life pushed him forward as if he could barely contain the happiness that had taken over not only his soul but his mind as well. The worries about poverty, which had held him back from making any plans, seemed to vanish suddenly that day as though he had grown wings. He felt that now he could break free from these miserable limitations and be liberated; he could soar into the splendor of this unexpected love. Surely, Faibiş wouldn't be pleased with what Dan had to tell him, but eventually, he would understand that Dan was being honest and that his love for Anişoara was mutual.

After speaking with the foreman Stoica and finishing his first morning rounds among the machines, Dan returned to the office. Anişoara looked at him from her desk with a bright smile and eager eyes, clearly happy to see him. On his desk, a small package, carefully wrapped in white paper and tied with a ribbon, awaited him. He looked at her, silently asking what it was. She simply replied,

"It's for you."

Dan opened the middle drawer of his desk, where he kept his paperwork for the day, placed Anișoara's package inside, and began untying the ribbon. Inside, between two pieces of confectioner's cardboard, he found a collection of homemade biscuits sprinkled with sugar, cut into various shapes resembling stars, crescent moons, and other geometric shapes. While she watched to gauge his reaction, Dan asked,

"They're still warm. When did you make them?"

"This morning. I woke up early. You know, neither sorrow nor joy lets you sleep..." She wanted to say love but held back, worried that Comrade Vintilă might be listening.

"Thank you! We'll eat them later. I want to go to the carpenter's shop first to talk to Faibiș." And with that, he left.

On the path behind the factory leading to the lake, the carpentry shop occupied a brick hall, its walls painted a yellow-brown color. The large rolling door, big enough for trucks to enter, was open, and Radu, the young man who sometimes covered for Faibiș when he wasn't there, came out to greet Dan.

"Morning, Dan. What brings you here?"

"I need to talk to Faibiș about something delicate."

"He's in the office. He's not in a good mood today."

Dan shrugged, "What I have to say won't make him any happier..."

When Dan entered the office, Faibiş stood up from his chair and suggested they go outside, where it was cooler. They stepped out onto the street, and Faibiş sat on the curb, pulling out a pack of cigarettes and offering one to Dan. Dan waved it away.

"I haven't smoked since I left the army."

"Anişoara is in love with you," Faibiş said, getting straight to the point. "She told me about it this morning on the way here. In a way, I'm glad she chose you and not someone else. I knew something like this was going to happen. I could never compete with her. She's stronger. I can't compete with you either. You're both tougher and stronger together. There's nothing I can do. She said you didn't want to kiss her before telling me. Like I said before, I'm glad she chose you."

With that, he stood up and offered his hand to Dan, who was left speechless by the honesty of this young man he had feared would cause him much trouble.

Back at the office entrance, Anişoara was waiting anxiously to hear the outcome of the conversation. Dan reassured her from the doorway raising his thumb towards the sky. She smiled, understanding the message. After lunch, Faibiş came to take Dan upstairs to the payroll office for salaries.

"Today is your first salary. You owe us a celebration!" Faibiş said.

"That will have to wait. I want to find something—a gift for Anişoara—and I don't know what to get her."

"If you're thinking of jewelry, a ring or something, I know a guy who deals in that kind of thing."

"That sounds like a good idea, but with my money, I'm not sure what I can get…"

"I'll call him and find out where you can meet. He'll give you a deal."

"You're amazing, Faibiş! Will you come with me?"

"We'll see. Maybe."

Before the workday ended, a crowd had gathered in front of Dan's office, waiting for their pay. The first confrontation came with Comrade Cocoi, who, upon seeing that he wasn't getting his usual amount, loudly announced for everyone to hear,

"I was going to suggest that you become a party member, but you're clearly against the working class!"

"I'm not against the working class, Comrade Cocoi! I'm against those who demand more than they deserve!"

"We'll see what the situation is with you! You'll see!"

"I don't have any problems. You do!" Dan replied firmly.

After the money was handed out, Faibiș came to get Dan.

"Where are we going?"

"To the racetrack."

"Are there races today?"

"No. Hurry up, the guy is waiting for us." They picked up the pace.

Near the ticket booth at the entrance to the stands, a man in a floral shirt, hat, and sunglasses was waiting. Holding a newspaper under his arm, he examined Dan from behind his shades before pulling a small pouch, like the kind from a pharmacy, out of his pocket. He poured a few golden items into his palm: two rings, a wedding band, a small gold watch without a strap specifically for women, and a silver crucifix with a chain. Dan focused on the crucifix. He held it in his palm, turned it over, and asked for the price. After some negotiation, Dan left the racetrack, parting from Faibiș and the man with that crucifix firmly clasped in his hand.

* * *

The next morning, when Dan entered the workshop to speak with the foreman Stoica, he was met by Comrade Decu, the lathe operator.

"You shortchanged me. You gave me a hundred lei less."

"That's impossible. You signed for it..."

"I signed, but you gave me less."

"I can't help you. I counted the money correctly." Dan turned to leave, but the man grabbed him by the arm.

"You won't get away with this! You'll give me my money! I'll kill for those hundred lei!"

"I don't have any extra money to give. Next time, be more careful!" Dan said, trying to shake him off.

A crowd gathered around them, and foreman Stoica stepped in, trying to convince Comrade Decu to handle the matter civilly in the office. Dan stormed off to his office, frustrated, followed by the foreman, the agitated lathe operator, and several workers.

"He's a gangster. Not only does he rob us on our payroll, but he also robs us blind. Imagine giving me a hundred lei less! When was that ever happened before? But it won't work with me! I'll strangle him! Mark my words!"

Just then, the engineer Decu, the lathe operator's brother, entered the office.

"What's going on here? What's all this commotion?"

"He shortchanged me a hundred lei last night on my salary," said the lathe operator.

"Give him the hundred back, and we'll put an end to this," the engineer told Dan.

"I didn't take any money from him. I counted everything correctly, and beyond that, I don't know what he did with the money," Dan replied.

"Yeah, but he says you didn't give him the full amount."

"He should've counted it here, in front of me..."

"But he did count it! I was here. I saw it!" Anișoara interjected from her desk.

"What did you see?" the engineer asked.

"He was sitting here, where he is now when he got the money. And Comrade Cocoi told him to count, saying Comrade Dan was stealing. And he counted."

"Was Comrade Cocoi here when this happened? Please call Cocoi," said the engineer.

"Yes!" the girl confirmed. "And he argued with Comrade Dan, too."

Comrade Cocoi entered the office.

"Were you here yesterday when Comrade Decu got his pay?" the engineer asked.

"Yes," the machinist replied.

"Did you see him count it?"

"I saw it."

"Now, what do you have to say?" the engineer asked his brother.

"I don't know. I don't remember," the lathe operator muttered.

"Get back to work, then. And you, be more careful with the money!" the engineer told his brother. "Enough with this nonsense!"

Dan sat at his desk, reflecting on the situation. Suddenly, it dawned on him: the lathe operator was upset about the hundred lei that was now missing from what he used to get after the adjustments to the norms from the worksheets. It was true that because of Dan, he received less. So that was the reason. He finally understood!

Anişoara turned off the speaker from which Maria Tănase had been pouring out the curses of her famous folk song. As she passed by Dan, she lightly brushed his shoulder, seemingly by accident, and Dan turned toward her as if awakened from a daze. The clear blue of her eyes absorbed his nervous tension, soothing him with their calming, balm-like effect. The office was now completely quiet. Engineer Decu had left, and Comrade Vintilă swiveled in his chair to speak softly to Dan.

"I don't like meddling in others' affairs, but I must tell you, as a friend, you've started a war here. I think you have more enemies than friends around you. Take it easy, I'm sincerely telling you, and be cautious—you're dealing with dangerous wolves. Especially those two from this morning." After a brief look into Dan's eyes, ensuring he understood, Comrade Vintilă returned to his work.

Before noon, the phone on Anişoara's desk rang. It was the secretary of Comrade Leontescu, the chief engineer of the plant.

"The comrade chief engineer would like to speak with Comrade Daniel Cristescu at two o'clock in his office."

Anişoara passed the message to Dan, remaining worried at his desk. It was now evident that things had escalated more than he expected. Dan pulled a lined notepad from his drawer and began quickly drawing columns on several pages. He placed a stack of worksheets on his desk and copied a series of numbers. Then, flipping through the pages he usually carried around the machines, he pulled out additional data to add to his lists. When everyone left for the lunch break, Dan, calm and confident, approached Anişoara with a small package wrapped in white paper and tied with a ribbon and handed it to her. She curiously glanced at his eagerness to see her reaction and then unwrapped the package. Inside a small box, coiled around a white card, was a silver chain with a beautiful cross hanging from it. Anişoara seemed touched by the gift, admiring it silently, then, covering the cross with her hands, she asked:

"You know I can never wear this cross, right?"

"It doesn't matter! This cross symbolizes my faith...in you. By keeping the cross, you keep me. More than that, it's our connection to the Holy Lord."

Anișoara took the cross from the box, wrapped it along with the card back in the white paper, retied the ribbon, and placed it near her heart inside her blouse.

"See? I can wear it. I'll always have it with me, and no one will criticize me."

Dan was more than satisfied. He felt the warmth of Anișoara's heart transmitted through the cross to his own. Nothing could diminish his inner joy that through this cross, he had found a symbolic bridge between their two hearts, now beating in unison.

Five minutes before the meeting, Dan entered the waiting room of Comrade Leontescu's office, the chief engineer, with a folder of paper in hand. The secretary invited him to take a seat and went in to announce his presence. A minute later, he was asked to enter.

"Good afternoon, Comrade Engineer," said Dan.

"You're Comrade Cristescu, the one everyone's talking about?" Dan nodded. "Word has reached me that you refuse to follow the orders of your superiors in your department."

"If you mean Comrade Engineer Decu, then yes, you're right," Dan said.

"Why, Comrade? Do you know who Comrade Decu is to us? Compared to him, you're nothing, a flea. Do you dare challenge such a man, Comrade? Go back, apologize, and let's not talk about this again! Go on, I've got work to do!"

"Please, with respect, let me explain," Dan tried to speak.

"What's there to explain? There's nothing to explain! You must do what you're told. Have you served in the army? It's the same here! Orders are to be followed!"

"Orders are followed, Comrade Chief Engineer. But you have the right to report violations of the law!" Dan countered.

The engineer, irritated, got up from his desk and approached Dan, shouting:

"What violations? What laws? Since when are you a legal expert? I'm telling you, get it into your head, or I'll toss you out like a rotten tooth!"

Dan also stood up.

"Please don't shout at me! I have the evidence of the violations," he said, holding up the folder.

"Do you think that I'll waste time debating this with you? Here, we have one law: you do what you're told! I'll transfer you to another section for disciplinary reasons. You can leave now. Go!" the engineer said, pointing to the door.

Dan realized there was nothing more to say. He left the office, dazed and bewildered. He could use a cigarette but had no one to ask. He wandered into the payroll office and asked the secretary if he could speak with Comrade Fazekaş, the head of the department. She received him immediately.

"How can I help you, Comrade Cristescu?"

Dan sat down and explained everything, showing her the table of quotas, he had worked on earlier.

"The problem is," he said, "that instead of 48 hours a week, we're paying for 60-70 hours without any productivity gains. If, after norms are recorded on the worksheets, a worker achieves less than 55 hours weekly, Engineer Decu adjusts the norm, so it appears they've completed more. This way, of course, he can boast that his workshop exceeds norms by an average of 170%. It's all bragging and deception."

Comrade Fazekaş listened without interrupting and then handed Dan some sheets of paper.

"Write all this down, black and white, in a statement, and leave it with me," she said. Dan complied, writing several pages.

When he entered his office, Dan realized the workday had

long since ended, and no one was there except Anișoara, who was anxiously waiting to hear how the meeting with Comrade Leontescu had gone. Dan sat down, overwhelmed, and said:

"I've been transferred to another section for disciplinary reasons. The burden will likely fall on your shoulders again. I've become as ridiculous and abandoned as Don Quixote, Cervantes' hero. You can't fight windmills—no one believes you!"

"No, Dan! You're not ridiculous, and you're not abandoned. If they make me do your job, I'll do it exactly like you! You are right, and justice must prevail! No Don Quixote and no windmills!"

She glanced through the window to see if anyone was still in the workshop, then moved closer to Dan, wrapping her arms around his shoulders as if in an embrace, and kissed him on his forehead.

* * *

The next day, Saturday, Dan had a longer conversation with Foreman Stoica, who attentively listened, nodding at what was being said. After making his rounds in the workshop, noting the operations at each machine, Dan returned to the office. During this time, Anișoara and Comrade Vintilă took their places at their desks, greeting him with a good morning. Dan stopped by the wall speaker and turned it on. The calm voice of Dorina Drăghici filled the room with the soft sounds of the popular melody "Firicel de floare albastră. (Little thread of bluey flower)"

Anişoara watched Dan with a smile, happy to see him in a better mood than the previous evening. He winked at her as he sat at his desk. He was glad it was Saturday and that tomorrow, a holiday, they could spend more time together. Both had so much to say to each other, but considering recent events, it seemed like a dense fog hovered around them, blocking the sunlight radiating from their souls. Some of the commitments she had made in the UTM (Union of Communist Youth) committee had been neglected lately. She had even missed one of the meetings and knew she would soon be harshly criticized for it. However, now she was happier than ever, and even her parents had noticed the change in her in recent days without knowing the cause. Only Emilia and another girl from the neighborhood knew her secret, and whenever they met, they would gossip and laugh together.

Anişoara had always been a happy child, full of optimism and surrounded by friends. She grew up free and lively, initiating and joining in on games with other children, climbing trees with the boys, often wrestling with them, filling the air with her voice and laughter, but never a scream. She was conscientious in school, always doing her homework keeping her notebooks neat, with round, legible handwriting and no random ink stains on the pages. She was always rewarded and recognized. Now, though, she seemed even more cheerful and lively than usual, but at the same time, more preoccupied with something, more absent-minded about what was happening around her. She gave the impression that her true experiences were happening somewhere deep inside her.

Before noon, the Personnel Office secretary entered the room, going straight to Anişoara and asking who Comrade Cristescu was. Anişoara pointed to Dan. The secretary handed him a sealed white envelope with no addressee and left. Dan opened it, pulled out a sheet of typed paper, and read it. He was informed that starting Monday the following week, he was being transferred as a disciplinary measure to the Supply Department. Dan passed the letter to Anişoara, who read it with bated breath and handed it back to him. Comrade Vintilă watched the exchange, and Dan handed him the letter from the envelope as well.

"I told you this would have consequences," he said, returning the letter.

From behind the partition window into the workshop, Comrade Decu, the lathe operator, had also been watching the envelope being passed from desk to desk, satisfied that things had progressed faster than he thought possible.

* * *

The day before, as they parted, Anişoara had told Dan to come to her house around two o'clock. On his way to the tram, he came across a woman on the Grant Bridge carrying a basket full of flowers, from whom he bought a splendid bouquet of white peonies.

Armed with these flowers, he arrived at his destination. He knocked on the brown-painted picket fence gate, and a man in a striped shirt with rolled-up sleeves came to open it. From behind him, around the corner of the house, Anişoara appeared, blushing, with her hand on the gate latch.

"Father, let me! This is him, Daniel. Daniel Cristescu, the friend I told you about last night."

With the gate open, Dan shook the outstretched hand of the man in front of him. Anişoara pulled him by the arm toward the back of the yard, paved with red bricks. Behind the large house, there were a few smaller rooms, one of which was the kitchen. Anişoara's mother came outside, too, wearing an apron and wiping her hands before Dan kissed them. With a radiant smile lighting up her face, Anişoara grabbed the flowers from his hand, saying:

"Let me put them in water!" Then, turning to her mother:

"May I take the big vase from the house?"

"Take it, my dear," her mother replied, somewhat embarrassed by her daughter's question. "We're almost done, and soon we'll set the table. Gică, take care of our guest!"

"Would you like to have a small glass of ţuică (plum brandy) with me?"

"With pleasure," Dan replied.

The two of them sat on a bench in the shade near the open kitchen window, where Anişoara's father brought a clay pitcher and two small glasses.

"You have a beautiful house," Dan said.

"Yes. My father built it. My grandfather had a strip of land in Mogoşoaia and five sons. When they decided to build the railway to Curtea de Argeş (a picturesque historical location), Prince Bibescu wouldn't allow the train to pass through his forests, so the line was diverted over the fields of the villagers on the edge of the commune. My grandfather's land was split in two by the train, and he could no longer plow from one end to the other. But my grandfather didn't give up. He knew a good lawyer from his army days and fought the Kingdom. He won. He split the money equally among his sons, and my father bought and built what you see here. I was born here, and this is where I want to die," said the man. "But where are you from?"

"From Ialomiţa. When my father was young, he was sent to the Eastern Front. When he returned, he had been shot in the shoulder, which left his right arm paralyzed. His other brother died in the front of Odessa. My father had some land, but he couldn't work it anymore, so he hired people from the village. When the regime changed, they said he was a kulak and took everything from him except for the house where he still lives. I wasn't allowed to finish school because of it, so I went to my aunt's place in Bucharest, the widow of my father's brother. She's struggling because they no longer give her the veteran's pension since her husband fought against Russia. My father still comes to visit her with his cart, bringing a sack or two of potatoes, wheat, whatever he has."

"Yes, it's tough, I understand! Let's go inside now; I see the women have almost finished their work here. Let's bring the țuică with us," said Anișoara's father, smiling as he pointed to the pitcher in his hand.

They entered the large house, climbing a few steps in front of a door that led to a room where the table was set with a starched tablecloth and plates. In the center, the flowers Dan had brought were placed in a painted porcelain vase. To the left and right of the room were doors leading to other rooms. The men sat across from each other at the table. Anișoara's father filled their glasses again, as did those of the women who were about to join them. Anișoara brought out an enameled bowl of soup. Her mother, holding the ladle, apologized, saying there hadn't been enough time to prepare a proper meal as would have been appropriate for such an occasion.

"Don't worry, Mother, Dănuț isn't one of those picky ones. He knows how to appreciate what's made with love," Anișoara said.

"I assure you; your hospitality impresses me beyond words. I wasn't prepared to meet such welcoming and open-hearted people on my first visit," Dan said.

"Let's drink to our health, all of us," Anişoara's father said. "Cheers!"

"Cheers!" the others repeated.

After the meal, Anişoara's parents retreated to their room, which faced the street. The girl began clearing the dishes and taking them to the kitchen, where she started washing them. Dan was given a towel to dry them, and he watched her swift movements, accustomed to the duties of a good homemaker. When they were finished, she asked him:

"Would you like to see my room?"

She led him back into the main house. It was a lovely room with polished furniture, a double bed in the center, two nightstands on either side, a dressing table with a mirror, and a large wardrobe. Pictures and a few paintings adorned the walls.

"Now go to the next room; I want to change. Shall we go to the park?"

"Let's go," Dan replied.

After a few minutes, she emerged in a light blue printed cotton dress with a square neckline and white sandals, matching the small clutch in her hand. She took Dan by the arm, and they stepped out onto the street. The sheer curtain on the street-facing window fluttered, moved by the breath of the softened parental hearts, who watched them admiringly.

From behind his fence, Faibiş saw them from his yard. He stepped to the gate and called out to them. They both stopped. Faibiş caught up with them.

"Where are you going?"

"To the park. Want to come with us?"

"No, what would I do between the two of you? I heard you've been transferred to Supply. The boss there, Comrade Carol, is a decent guy. You'll like it. He's helped a lot of people," Faibiş said.

"The problem is, what am I supposed to do in Supply?"

"Don't worry, you'll figure it out. I caught Comrade Decu yesterday during the day, asleep in the locker room, slumped over the cabinets. He reeked of booze. That's how he's breaking the norms! Interesting, huh? He didn't even notice me when I walked past him. I've seen him drinking from a mess tin before, but I didn't pay attention."

Anişoara pulled away from Dan, outraged:

"You didn't call someone as a witness? You should have gone to the Party and caught him red-handed!"

"There's no point with these people. They cover for each

other, and it's the innocent ones like us who get pushed down. None of them are any better. All talk, that's all…"

"You're probably right," Dan said. "There's nothing to be done!"

They parted ways with Faibiş, reflecting on the information they had just received. They walked silently for a while. Anişoara pulled Dan toward a street that cut more directly toward the lake, and in the shady grove of trees lining the path around the lake, they found an empty bench with sunlight filtering through the leaves. They sat down next to each other, and Dan wrapped an arm around Anişoara's shoulders, gently caressing her neck. He felt something around her neck and suddenly turned to face her. Only now did he realize she was wearing his little cross. It shimmered subtly above the square neckline of her dress, almost blending in with the porcelain-like whiteness of her skin, making the discovery of the cross nearly impossible. An instinctive impulse made him kiss her hand first, then her lips, this wonderful girl who never ceased to surprise him with her tenderness and displays of affection, which he wasn't sure he deserved. Anişoara pulled away from his embrace, looking at him slightly puzzled:

"I told you I would never part with it! You didn't believe me?"

"I did. But now you've shown it to the world…"

"Not the whole world. Just you!" And then, it was her turn to kiss him.

* * *

The next morning, Anișoara walked into the mechanical workshop to gather the attendance sheets and saw Comrade Stoica approaching her with a rat trap in hand. Looking closer, she noticed a crushed rat trapped under the arched mechanism of the device.

"What are you going to do with it?" she asked.

"I'll feed it," the foreman replied.

He placed the trap on his desk, took a small box from a drawer containing a white powder, and removed the rat from the trap, holding it in his hand. With a spoon from the box, he scooped a small amount of the substance and forced it into the rat's mouth. Within seconds, the poor animal was dead in his hand.

"What is that?" Anișoara asked.

"Sodium cyanide. We sometimes use it in welding. It's the most powerful poison."

"Could you give me some? I have mice in the storeroom, and I can't get rid of them."

"No. No one touches this stuff but me. You saw that I keep it locked away. This can kill a person in two minutes."

"Comrade Stoica, just a little, to sprinkle in the corners of the storeroom…"

"No!"

"Please. I'll take care of it myself. I won't let anyone else handle it. Just a bit…"

"Get yourself a cat!" the foreman said, locking the box back in the drawer. "Children shouldn't play with things like this."

"A cat won't help. They keep coming back."

"Fine. I'll prepare a diluted solution in a small bottle for you. Pour it into the holes where they appear."

"Thanks! That'll do. You know what I want now? I want to continue the work Comrade Cristescu started. I want to track the real-time spent on each operation from the technological sheets. Will you help me?"

"I talked with him about it on Saturday. There's no need for you to come here. I'll give you a list at the end of each day with the exact times. Happy now?"

"Oh yes! You're a gem. Thank you!" Anișoara said, walking away.

Meanwhile, Dan was in the procurement office, waiting near the secretary of Comrade Carol. The room was spacious, filled with desks, all occupied by clerks, many engaged in long phone conversations; on the wall opposite the window, which overlooked the inner courtyard, framed photos of Khrushchev and Gheorghiu-Dej loomed, flanked by the crossed flags of Romania and the Soviet Union.

At one point, a small man in a gray suit and tie entered, heading straight for the door to the adjacent room. The secretary stood up and followed him. A moment later, she reappeared at the door, gesturing for Dan to come in.

Comrade Carol fixed his gaze on Dan, his forehead glistening with sweat, under bushy eyebrows, his sharp blue eyes focused intently.

"Have a seat," he said. Dan sat across from him.

"The comrades in Human Resources say you're dangerous and that I should keep an eye on you. Are you dangerous?"

Dan smiled. "Maybe I am if that's what they say... but I don't think so."

"I don't think so either. Have you worked in procurement before?"

"No. And I don't understand why a technician was assigned here?"

"Well, if he's dangerous as a technician, where should we put him? Here! But, comrade, this is no easy job. Here, it's a battle!

For every material, you must fight. You need a plan, a strategy. And you need resources. Do you have resources?"

"I don't. I don't even know what that means," Dan admitted.

"Without resources, you won't get far. Do you know what emulsion is?"

"Emulsion is a mixture of water and oil used in cutting machines for cooling and lubricating tools."

"Something like that. You're close. Is it a basic product? No. If it's not basic, then why does it cause such headaches? Can you tell me?"

"I don't know," Dan answered, smiling. This guy's got a sense of humor, he thought.

"Watch this," Carol continued, picking up the phone. "Comrade Manole, please... Hi, Carol here. Yes, I've wanted to talk to you for a while... Oh, the usual: troubles, headaches, worries, when will we be rid of them? Tell me, that emulsion order for 10 barrels. The month is nearly over, and we still haven't received them. Not five, ten. Why only five? What do you expect me to do, shut down the production? You said you'd investigate it… What? Three meters of white silk? Your daughter's wedding? I understand… And a demijohn of wine? I don't know, I'll see… but I'm counting on those ten barrels. Fine. I'll send the truck on

Friday."

Comrade Carol wiped his forehead with a handkerchief.

"See how easily materials are procured? But that's not all. Watch this…" He dialed another number: "Comrade Ionescu. How are you? I heard you were sick. Glad it wasn't worse. Yes, we must take care of ourselves. Listen, I need your help with something serious—a material I need. No, no, it's nothing big, just six meters of white silk. It's for a wedding, not mine, for the guy with the material. What do you say? Two packs of Chesterfields? What, Camels aren't good enough anymore? Maybe some Kents? No, only Chesterfields? With filters, I understand. I'll try... by Thursday… Okay, take care. "

The man in front of Dan looked exhausted.

"I never imagined situations like this," Dan remarked. "It's worse than I expected."

"Worse? Who says it's worse? Wait until you see how things are with raw materials! That's where the real battle is fought life or death. You can't shut down the plant! For a ton of material, they'll ask for a forest and two castles on top of it. That's the real test. This emulsion business is just like Comrade Caragiale (a Romanian writer dead two decades before) said: 'The chain of weaknesses."

"But what about planning? The big Five-Year Plan?"

"On paper, my friend. Only on paper!"

* * *

After entering the office, engineer Decu asked Anişoara if she had taken care of the payroll list. The girl got up from her desk to hand it to him and then returned to her place. As usual, Comrade Decu reached into his jacket pocket to grab his pen for corrections:

"Comrade Murguleanu, the tech sheets, please," the boss requested.

"No need, comrade engineer. No one worked fewer than fifty-five hours last week," Anişoara replied.

The engineer looked at her, surprised:

"What? And now you're starting to contradict me?"

"No, not at all. But every worker in the workshop is getting 30-60 percent over their base salary. Of the others, no one gets a penny more than their salary, except for those working on norms. I think there's a limit to this, too, right?"

"How do you know they get 30-60 percent more?"

"I have here the list prepared by Comrade Cristescu with the hours worked. It's quite revealing."

"May I see it?" Anişoara handed it to him. The engineer glanced over it, then tore it to pieces and threw the scraps into the trash bin.

"This is what you're basing your claims on? It's garbage!"

"The 'garbage' you're talking about was verified by Comrade Stoica. I have copies prepared from this list for the District Party Committee and the Scânteia (The Spark) newspaper. You can do what you want, but I will personally submit them!"

"I understand. There's no need to take them! I thought you were a smart girl, but I see that this Comrade Cristescu has turned you into a she-wolf. Take the list to payroll."

Anişoara returned to her desk. The engineer seemed engrossed in resolving some papers that had been sitting on his desk for quite some time while Comrade Vintilă, completely detached from what had just happened, was entering sums from his papers into a register.

At the end of the workday, Anişoara stayed behind in the office, knowing that Dan wouldn't be late in showing up. Faibiş no longer came around like he used to, asking if she was heading home because now Dan was the one walking her home. Instead, the mornings were Faibiş's. He still waited for her, as before, by the edge of the sidewalk near the fence of his house so they could walk to the plant together. Since Dan had entered her life, Faibiş seemed more relaxed, less interested in finding out who she had spoken to when he wasn't with her, and much more reserved. Anişoara, however, just as before, would tell him everything without holding back—about what she did or planned to do, about Dan, with whom she got along wonderfully, and even about certain contradictory discussions she had with other people. In turn, Faibiş would tell her the latest jokes, some juicy gossip circulating among the people, and his plans for a September fishing trip in the Danube Delta.

The workshop lights had gone out, and Foreman Stoica, now changed out of his work clothes, entered the office to hand over the promised list of today's execution times and a small bottle wrapped in paper. He looked at Anişoara without saying anything, making a gesture with his index finger, signaling her to take notice. After he left, Dan came into the office and pulled his chair from his desk closer to hers, sitting face to face.

"How was your day?" Anişoara asked. "Did you miss me?"

"Don't ask. But I couldn't think too much about you. This comrade Carol is smart; he talks straight, like the people in our village, and cracks jokes that you can't help but laugh at. I spent the whole day with him in his office. I have a lot to learn from him. But I don't know if I could do what he does. He walks a fine line. Everything he does is with the most honorable intentions, but if someone rats him out, he'll go to prison for life. You know what he told me? He said this problem is, like Comrade Caragiale put it, 'the chain of weaknesses.'" Dan laughed. She laughed, too.

"But how was your day without me?"

"Abandoned. I threatened Comrade Decu that I'd go to the Party and to Scânteia to show them how he's setting the work norms. He backed down. He said you turned me into a she-wolf."

Dan laughed, satisfied:

"Come here, my dear she-wolf, so I can kiss you! I didn't turn you into a she-wolf. You already were one; you just didn't know it. Now you know, and that's why I love you."

"Because I'm a she-wolf?"

"Because the wolf is a noble animal. It's loyal, just, and loves its cubs. And no one steals from its bowl. The fox is cunning. You have to watch out for it," Dan said, holding her hands in his.

"You're a fox. I know you. I see you. I can smell you. You're telling me I'm a she-wolf just to get under my skin. But it's not going to work, Fox. Let's go now. Are you taking me home?"

"No."

"Why not?"

"Because I'm a fox trying to get under your skin."

"You won't get under unless I let you. Let's go, fox."

* * *

When Comrade Engineer Decu entered the office, Anişoara

informed him that Comrade Fazekaş from the Labor and Wages Department requested that he call her, as she wished to speak with him. The engineer immediately picked up the receiver and dialed the number. Fazekaş asked if he could come to discuss something with her, and Comrade Decu went right away.

"Comrade Engineer, who prepares the technological sheets in the mechanical workshop?" Fazekaş asked.

"I do."

"And the work norms?"

"I also do. Is there something wrong?" the engineer inquired.

"No, not at all. I just want to clarify something for my understanding. By what criteria do you set the norms?"

"From experience, Comrade Fazekaş. As you probably know, I used to be a lathe operator at Grivița Roşie. I know the technological process well, and I have a lot of experience."

"Agreed. But your lathe from Grivița Roşie, did it change speeds automatically, or did it have a stepped pulley?"

"No, at that time, very few lathes had gearboxes."

"Could the automatic speed change influence execution time?" the payroll chief asked again.

Beads of sweat began to form on the engineer's forehead.

"I don't understand where you're going with this, comrade… Anything can change the time. A simple tool with widia inserts has a different yield than a rapid steel tool. Of course, yes."

"I believe you're not considering that nearly twenty years have passed since you last worked at Grivița Roșie. Things have evolved and so have the norms."

"That's not true. I've also worked in the Soviet Union…"

"In the Soviet Union, you were given six months to complete your exam pieces. You didn't work in the factory side by side with other workers who had to meet their norms. But there's another issue. I have information that you modify the norms in the technological sheets after the parts are produced. Is this true?"

The engineer pulled a handkerchief from his jacket pocket to wipe his forehead.

"Comrade Fazekaș, I feel like you're questioning me as if I were a criminal. You forget that I'm a veteran of the socialist cause who was imprisoned for it. You cannot…"

"Comrade Decu! Yes, you were imprisoned, I know, but not because you faced the gendarmes' bullets in 1933. You weren't even there in 1933. You were accepted into the Party only in 1947. Let's not confuse the facts. Now, in conclusion, you will no longer be in charge of setting the norms. I will place someone there who will handle it scientifically. I believe we understand each other," Comrade Fazekaş said, standing up.

"I think you're judging me too harshly. The majority of workers in the mechanical workshop are first-class professionals. You can see that in all the results so far. Come and see for yourself, and you'll be convinced!"

"I don't deny that. What I don't accept is favoritism. We do not alter the norms to boast about top workers, especially when it causes the plant to lose tens of thousands of lei by inflating wages. Goodbye!"

Upon returning to his office, Engineer Decu fixed Anişoara with a frown, suspecting that she must have been the one who went to report him to Comrade Fazekaş and who knows where else. He now deeply regretted allowing himself to be deceived by her beauty and apparent naivety and not firing her much earlier. But now it was too late, and this situation could overturn everything he had built over the years. His mind raced, trying to figure out what could still be done to get rid of her. Having her as a thorn in his side in this office was not a solution. The bad part was that everyone knew and respected her as a good worker, a member of the institution UTC Committee, and with connections at the District Party and UTC upper levels. Even if he tried to accuse her of some wrongdoing, no one would believe him, and he would only risk damaging his own credibility. So, what should he do?

* * *

The next day after payday, during the lunch break on his way to the cafeteria, Comrade Cocoi opened the door to the office where Anişoara was alone. Without stepping inside, he asked her if she could check whether everything was prepared in the meeting room for the after-hours Party Committee meeting. She replied that she would check, and he asked her to stop by his machine to get the key to the room. After resuming work, Anişoara went to Comrade Cocoi to collect the key and then continued her way toward the auxiliary stairwell, where the meeting room for the mass organizations of the technical service was located. She opened the door and looked inside: opposite the entrance stood the podium with two steps and the presidium table, covered in a red cloth, with a jug of water, several glasses on a tray, and several chairs facing the assembly. The rest of the room was furnished with chairs arranged in rows and a metal cabinet from which she took notebooks and pencils, placing them neatly on the table atop the podium.

While she was busy with these tasks, Comrade Decu, the lathe operator, entered the room. After closing the door, he approached her menacingly on the podium without saying a word, clearly intent on doing something. Suspicious, Anişoara looked at him, trying to discern his intentions. He was twice her size and strength. She instinctively tried to keep a safe distance between them. He followed her, grabbed her by the waist, and with one hand on the back of her neck, bent her over the red cloth of the table. Anișoara struggled, kicking and waving her arms as she cried and screamed:

"No, Comrade Decu! Please, no, Comrade Decu!"

But he was unleashed, not hearing a word. He grabbed the back of her neck with both hands and smashed her head against the tabletop several times. Holding her down with one hand, he lifted the hem of her dress with the other, tugged down her underwear with force, and entered her body like a bulldozer. When he was done, he turned her over to face him. She was still. He laid her on the floor behind the table, bashing her head twice more against the thick edge of the table's support leg before leaving.

As Decu passed by Comrade Cocoi's milling machine on his way back to the shop, he answered Cocoi's questioning glance by slowly lowering his eyelids, signaling that everything was in order. After Decu reached his machine, Cocoi set his own machine to automatic mode and headed for the back exit of the workshop. He found Anișoara sobbing, sitting with her legs curled beneath her, leaning against the table leg with her face bloodied. Seeing him, she whimpered through her tears:

"Comrade Decu. Look what Comrade Decu did to me..."

Cocoi walked to the door, opened it, and checked if anyone was nearby before locking it. He returned to Anișoara and told her to open her mouth while unfastening his trousers.

"Open your mouth, can't you hear?"

The girl sat with her mouth clenched shut, her eyes wide with terror. Cocoi slapped her mercilessly across the face, back and forth.

"Open your mouth, you filthy whore! What, you only do it with that layabout Cristescu? Open your mouth!"

A punch to her mouth was meant to break her resistance. When she still wouldn't comply, he grabbed her hair and pinched her nose shut. Gasping for air, the girl finally opened her mouth and holding her by the hair with one hand, Cocoi smugly continued with his plan. Afterward, he laid her out on the floor of the podium, lifting the hem of her dress over her face, now disfigured by blood and bruises, and took pleasure in her unresponsive body. When he finished, he considered strangling her for safety. But then he worried someone might discover fingerprints on her neck, so he changed his plan. He needed something solid to finish the job. Not finding anything suitable nearby, he noticed some bronze trophies on a shelf in the corner and grabbed one. Returning to the girl, he struck her head several times with the trophy, then wiped it with her dress and tossed it to the floor. Unlocking the door, he checked the scene and left for his machine. He waited anxiously for time to pass. Was she still alive? Would she speak? He had to go back and check on the situation.

When Cocoi returned and cracked open the door to the room, he saw that it was quiet. The girl was still in the same position he had left her. She was dead. Now, he could sound the alarm. He rushed, appearing distraught, to the foreman Stoica and told him he had found Anişoara dead. The foreman hurried along with Cocoi to the meeting room.

"Run to the infirmary," Stoica told Cocoi, "and bring a doctor here!"

"But she's dead," Cocoi muttered.

"Run! Don't you hear? Hurry!"

Cocoi left. The foreman remained with Anişoara, trying to feel for a pulse. It seemed he detected a faint throb in the jugular vein. It was a good sign, but the help they were waiting for was slow to arrive. He dashed to the office and told the only person present, Comrade Vintilă, to call for an ambulance and the police.

"But what happened?" asked Vintilă.

"Anişoara was attacked. It's serious!"

"Is she alive?"

"Yes! Make the call!" Stoica ran back to the girl.

Shortly after, Cocoi returned with a doctor from the infirmary. The doctor checked her heartbeat with a stethoscope, lamenting that he hadn't brought a stretcher to transport her. Without hesitating, Stoica lifted the girl in his arms and rushed her to the infirmary. The doctor and Cocoi followed closely behind. The ambulance and the police arrived at almost the same time. After learning that Anișoara had been taken to the infirmary, they went there too. Outside, a crowd had gathered, comrades from the UTM and Party Committee, even the head of personnel, eager to start an investigation.

Inside, Doctor Herșcovici, aided by two medical assistants, was trying to stabilize her vitals and somehow revive her. One of the nurses, while removing Anișoara's dress, found a small silver cross tied to her bra strap. Carefully, she unfastened it and placed it around Anișoara's neck. The girl began to mutter agitatedly:

"No! No, please don't!" and then fell silent again. The nurse started to cry.

In the workshop, a police officer in uniform and two plainclothes detectives began questioning the witnesses. The first to be interrogated was Comrade Vintilă, who had made the call to the police. After reporting everything he knew, he was asked to step out of the office to make room for the next person, Comrade Decu, the lathe operator.

"What do you know about this incident?" the officer asked.

"Well, what should I know? I know what everyone knows," the lathe operator replied calmly.

"What do you mean?"

"I know the comrade went to see Comrade Cocoi to get the key to the room so she could meet up with her boyfriend there."

"She has a boyfriend. Who is he?"

"Some new guy, been here about three-four weeks. His name's Cristescu."

"Is he here? Where can we find him?"

"No. He's not here anymore. He now works in Supplies."

The officer turned to one of the civilians.

"Comrade, could you go and bring this Comrade Cristescu here?"

The man got up and left.

"But how do you know it was Comrade Cristescu who committed the crime?" the officer asked Decu.

"I don't know that he committed the crime, but I know that's why she asked for the key to the room. See? So, who else could it have been? Eh?" The lathe operator was finally satisfied with his logic, which seemed to stump the officer.

"But how do you know she was supposed to meet him? Did she tell you, or someone else, that she was meeting him?"

"No. But didn't I see him hanging around earlier?"

"Where? Around here?"

"Well, around. Near the cafeteria!"

"Hmm. Wait a minute. To go from the cafeteria to the meeting room, he would have to pass through this workshop, right?"

"Well, yes, pretty much. But I saw him there," the lathe operator said, now feeling cornered himself.

"Why don't you ask the others outside if anyone saw him pass through the workshop?"

Comrade Decu went out into the hallway to ask. Meanwhile, the man sent to Supplies to fetch Cristescu had returned. The lathe operator re-entered the office.

"Did you find Comrade Cristescu?" the officer asked.

"No, Comrade Captain. He left early this morning on an assignment."

"Where to?"

"He left with a truck to Ploieşti to bring back some imucie."

"To bring back what?"

"Imucie, that's what the comrades at Supplies said. But I went to the auto section to check. He left at seven this morning."

"What do you make of that?" the officer now asked the lathe operator.

"I don't know. I think he's lying. I know I saw him."

"Did you talk to him?"

"No. We're not friends. He shorted me a hundred on my paycheck."

"When was this?"

"Two weeks ago."

"Alright. Go and tell the people that no one is allowed to leave until we finish the investigation here," said the captain. "Send in the next one!"

* * *

Among the crowd gathered in front of the infirmary was Faibiş. When he heard about Anişoara, a shock went through his heart. He had rushed over, desperate to be inside with his lifelong friend, for whom no sacrifice would have been too great or too costly. But he wasn't allowed in, and from the nurses, he could only get bits and pieces of news—that she was alive but in critical condition. He found comrade Stoica, the mechanic foreman, sitting grimly on a chair. Faibiş approached him. The foreman's shirt had bloodstains on the chest and sleeves from carrying the girl to the infirmary.

"Did you see her?" asked Faibiş.

"I was the one who brought her here."

"How was she?"

"Dead. Or almost dead. I didn't think she had any chance. She was unrecognizable. He violated her and then tried to get rid of her—may God strike him down!"

Hearing this, Faibiş was overcome by tears he struggled to hold back.

"Do you think it was someone from the workshop?"

"I don't know. Maybe. A lot has been happening here lately. Who knows? The thief gets one sin, but the victim bears ten. I can't figure anything out," the foreman concluded. "On the way here, in her agony, she kept saying, 'No, comrade Decu. No, comrade Decu.' Who knows what was on her mind…"

Faibiş wiped his tears with the back of his hand and walked away, ashamed.

Meanwhile, Dan had returned from Ploiesti with the ten barrels of emulsion and went straight to report to his new office. Comrade Carol was pleased to see him and informed him that the police were looking for him. Handing him an envelope from

Personnel, he also told him that as of Monday, Dan was being reassigned back to the mechanical workshop as a work planner. Dan smiled, pretending to wipe sweat from his brow, and said:

"Ah! Don't you feel, comrade Carol, that the world spins too fast in this speed-driven century? Two transfers and a promotion in the same week? Must be because I'm dangerous…"

"You know what they say: God's ways are mysterious! I'm sorry to see you go. Just be careful it's not a trap. Now go report to Personnel that you're back." Dan left.

A clerk from Personnel was assigned to go with Dan down to the mechanical workshop. Once there, he went straight to the captain to inform him that comrade Cristescu had returned. Dan was immediately called into his former office. The captain asked him:

"Are you comrade Cristescu?" Dan nodded.

"Where were you today around one o'clock?"

"I believe I was on the road back from Ploiesti."

"What business did you have in Ploiesti?"

"I was picking up ten barrels of emulsion for the factory."

"What time did you leave?"

"At seven in the morning."

"Well, some comrades claim they saw you here later. Do you

have witnesses that you were there?"

"Of course. Comrade Mihăilă, the driver. We were together the whole time."

"Go and bring comrade Mihăilă," the captain ordered his subordinate.

"Tell me, do you know comrade Anișoara Murguleanu?"

"Of course. What about her?"

"She was attacked."

"What? Where is she now? Is she alive?"

"For now, yes. She's in critical condition. What's your relationship with her?" the officer asked, studying the young man's reaction.

"She's, my fiancée."

"When did you last see her?"

"Last night, at her parents' house. Comrade Captain, please, I beg you, tell me where she is now. I need to see her. I'm at your disposal, but please, let me see her. I beg you!"

"I'm sorry you can't see her. She's in a coma!"

"In a coma? God, where is she?"

"At the infirmary. But they won't let you in. Calm down. We

need to find the criminal. Do you have any suspicions?"

"I don't know… maybe a few. All this happened because of me. I tried to fix a serious situation here, and now others are paying the price. It's all my fault… If I lose Anişoara, my life won't matter anymore. I'm the criminal in this case."

Dan, overwhelmed by guilt and pain for his beloved, the only true love of his life, seemed broken at the end of his endurance. The officer saw his condition and decided to suspend the interrogation, realizing there was nothing more to be gained. He stood up from his desk and helped Dan rise from his chair and exit into the corridor. There were many people still waiting to be questioned, and the captain was frustrated that he hadn't yet found the culprit.

When Dan got to exit the office, one of the people outside the door, comrade Decu, rushed at him with clenched fists, ready to attack him. But the captain quickly intervened and told him to come back into the office:

"Now, tell me again, where did you say you saw comrade Cristescu today?"

"I already told you, near the pastry shop."

"And what time was that?"

"I don't know… Must've been around 10 or 11."

"And when did comrade Murguleanu ask for the key to the

room?"

"I think it was after lunch. That's what I remember."

"Now, explain to me what you were doing at the pastry shop at ten o'clock. Were you on break?"

"No, comrade. I wasn't going to the pastry shop. I was heading to the locker room."

"During work hours? And who else did you see?"

"I don't know. I don't think I saw anyone else. I just saw comrade Cristescu."

"Where were you, and where was he when you saw him?"

"Well, you see, our corridor is quite dark. I was in the corridor, and he was in front of the pastry shop, in the light. That's how it was."

"Was he going in or coming out of the pastry shop?"

"Uh… I don't know."

"Was he facing the pastry shop or turned away from it?"

"I think he was… facing away. Yes, he was turned away."

"And then what happened?"

"What could've happened? I kept walking, and he went…"

"He went where? Did he pass by you?"

"No. He went… that way…"

"And where could 'that way' lead him? Toward the administration or the locker room?"

"I don't remember. What do you want from me? Why all these questions? I thought I was helping!"

"You help when you tell the truth. Take the comrade to Personnel to give a full statement with time, place, and people he saw or thinks may have seen him," the captain ordered his subordinate. "Now, go with the comrade and make a statement!"

"I can't. I need to go home. I've got a wife and kids. I wanted to help! Why won't you let me go home?"

The captain signaled for the agent to take him. At that moment, he was informed that comrade Mihăilă, the driver, was waiting outside. Mihăilă was called into the office.

* * *

After the captain saved Dan from the wrath of the lathe operator, Dan took a moment to collect himself. He gathered his strength and headed toward the infirmary, where his beloved was fighting for her life. Many of those gathered at the infirmary's door had left, but among those who remained, he found Faibiş and foreman Stoica. He read the worry on their faces and, without saying a word, sat down beside them. From the corridor, they tried to steal a glimpse of what was happening behind the white window cover, where shadows moved about like figures behind a sieve. At one point, Dan asked Faibiș if Anișoara's parents had been notified. Faibiș shook his head, and Dan decided to go inform them:

"Stay with her until I get back," Dan said before he left.

Outside, the sun was setting. Dan wished he could split in two: one part to stay with Anișoara in the infirmary and the other to bring the sorrowful news to her parents, who might not have another chance to see her alive. When he arrived, her worried parents asked in unison where Anișoara was. Dan didn't want to frighten them with a grim expression, but he couldn't muster joy either. He pulled her father aside and whispered the tragic news. Sensing something terrible, Anișoara's mother began to cry, not yet knowing why. Her father embraced her shoulders and said they needed to get dressed—Anișoara was in the hospital. They made the sad journey to the infirmary in complete silence.

* * *

Foreman Stoica was the first to be allowed into the room. The beds were lined up in two rows, reserved for the women. Led to Anișoara's bed, he was shocked to see her disfigured face swollen with bruises and her head entirely bandaged. She appeared to be resting after the day's traumatic events, and Stoica was somewhat reassured by her steady breathing, hoping that the worst had passed. He gently squeezed her hand, which lay stretched along her body over the blanket. Not wanting to disturb her, he stayed a few moments before leaving.

When Faibiş was granted permission to enter, he broke down into inconsolable tears, looking at his beloved friend, whom he couldn't recognize, as he felt miserable, helpless, and sorry. He sat on the edge of the bed, holding her hand, caressing it as he tried to comprehend what had happened in the few hours since they had last met. Anişoara sensed him, opened her bloodshot, terrified eyes, and whispered:

"No, Comrade Decu. No, Comrade Decu! No, please, no..."

Faibiş knelt beside her bed, continuing to hold her hand.

"Anişoara, it's me, Faibiş. Talk to me. Tell me, what happened?"

The girl kept crying.

"No, Comrade Decu. No, Comrade Decu. No..."

A nurse came to inform Faibiş that a police officer wanted to speak with Anişoara, and he had to leave. Faibiş protested.

"Didn't you tell them she can't speak?"

"Yes, but they must do their duty."

When the captain entered the room, Anișoara was still murmuring, "No, Comrade Decu. No, Comrade Decu..."

Upon seeing the girl, the captain immediately decided to assign an officer to guard her around the clock. The attacker might try once again to take her life. He inquired about the doctor who had admitted her and requested to speak with him. Dr. Herșcovici explained her condition, detailing the injuries that spread across most of her body, particularly the numerous blows to her skull with a hard object. At present, the patient was suffering from a concussion, aggravated by the trauma she had endured, along with the fact that she had been sexually assaulted by at least two individuals. The captain took note of all this.

When Dan and her parents arrived at the infirmary, no one was waiting outside of the infirmary door. Dan knocked on the door, and a nurse came to open it. He told her he was there with Anișoara's parents. The nurse tried to convince them that it was against the rules to allow visits after hours. Anișoara's mother wept, hiding her face in a handkerchief, and the nurse, moved by compassion, agreed to let only her in. Mr. Murguleanu insisted on going in as well to offer physical and emotional support to both his wife and his daughter, who had been through a terrible trauma. Understanding, the nurse led them to go to the girl's bedside while Dan remained outside.

Ever since learning of the attack on Anişoara, Dan's mind had been trying to review all the people who might have had an interest in committing such a barbaric act against a defenseless girl. Although there were some unpleasant characters in the workshop, he couldn't imagine any of them capable of such a deed. He still did not know what had happened the day before or how Anişoara ended up in that isolated room, but he thought there were only two possibilities: either she went there voluntarily and was followed by someone who forced their way in, or she didn't go willingly and was coerced. Which of these possibilities was true? From what he'd heard, he could tell that the situation was dire: Anişoara had suffered life-threatening injuries, and it was a miracle that she was still alive.

Meanwhile, the nurse had brought Anişoara's parents from the ward. They were emotionally shattered, supporting each other so they wouldn't collapse on the way back down the corridor. Dan helped them sit on the chairs by the wall. Mr. Murguleanu told him:

"She's delirious. She keeps repeating the engineer's name, repeating, 'No, Comrade Decu, no, Comrade Decu,' over and over."

When the nurse was about to leave, Dan looked at her with pleading eyes to let him see Anişoara, too. In the end, she couldn't resist the urge to act kindly and led him to the girl's bed. Anişoara was still agitated, continually murmuring, "No, Comrade Decu," but when she saw Dan, her distress intensified with signs of defense and rejection, flailing her arms and shouting:

"No! Not him, no. Go away! Leave! You can't be here. Go away!"

Seeing her reaction, the frightened nurse quickly pulled Dan out of the room and then, returning to the girl, tried to calm her down. Her bloodshot eyes were swimming in tears. Dan sat back down on one of the chairs in the corridor, holding his head in his hands. Anişoara's parents had left, but Mr. Murguleanu's words continued to echo in his mind. Engineer Decu? Could he be the cause of this tragedy? Why does Anişoara keep repeating his name? And why is she rejecting him?

He felt the need to think, but not there. The best thoughts come while you're walking alone, undisturbed by people or events. So, he left.

The infirmary was in the opposite wing from the administrative building and was dedicated to employees of the plant who suffered minor work accidents or illnesses that could be treated more quickly here than in a hospital. In the days following the attack, Anişoara showed only slight signs of improvement; she continued to appear terrified of anyone's presence, refused food, and required sedatives to be calmed. Each day between 5 and 7 pm, Anişoara's parents, Faibiş and Dan, would come to the infirmary, waiting to be admitted into the women's ward, where they were allowed only a few minutes to see her. Her reaction to these visits was cold and distant, and she didn't seem to recognize any of them, except for Dan, whom she avoided with gestures of rejection.

* * *

Monday morning, Dan returned to the office of the mechanical workshop, resuming his previous duties. Comrade Stoica was glad to see him and asked for news about Anişoara, whom he hadn't seen since the day of the attack. Few of the workers seemed happy to see him back, but Dan gave no indication that he cared about the coldness with which they looked at him. In the office, Comrade Vintilă also asked about their colleague and, turning confidentially toward Dan, said:

"I don't understand one thing: why was Comrade Engineer absent from work last Friday, and why, when he came in on Saturday morning, didn't he even ask why Comrade Murguleanu was missing? Doesn't that strike you as a bit odd?"

Dan remained thoughtful. "So, on the day of the attack, Engineer Decu was absent from work. Why? Could it be because he knew what was going to happen? And if, let's say, he knew, could he have stayed away to avoid any suspicion? Is this why Anişoara keeps mentioning his name? Because he might have called her to meet him there? How could the engineer have reached that room without being seen by anyone? It wasn't possible through the workshop. But if he went to another floor, he could have descended the auxiliary staircase where almost no one would have seen him. He knew he would find Anişoara there, waiting for him, and attacked her. So, who else could have committed this assault? Only Engineer Decu! But why? That's the question: Why all this, for what reason? First of all, why was he brought back into this office? Who brought him there? The Personnel Department? No way. Comrade Fazekaş, who told him to write that statement? Possibly. Because of his statement, he's back in this office, and Engineer Decu, to take revenge, attacked Anişoara. That's the reason!"

"I think I've solved the mystery," Dan told himself. "I need to talk to the militia captain!"

He hurriedly filled in the payroll sheets with the figures provided by Anişoara and Master Stoica, then delivered them to the Payroll Office. Now, he could head to the local militia office. On the way, he stopped by Faibiş's shop but didn't find him, so he continued his way.

The captain received Dan immediately, and he explained the reasons the attack was committed. He answered two or three questions the officer had before returning to his office. By the time he got back, it was past lunchtime, and he went to discuss some specifications with Master Stoica. Comrade Decu's lathe had been idle for a while, and the master was displeased that the department head's brother was taking too much advantage of his position. Dan asked the master whether he thought it would be better to time the work with laborers of different skill levels or with those of the same category. The master promised to think about it, mentioning that Dan might find the answer in his school notes. The new standards had to be established on a completely scientific basis.

As Dan was leaving the workshop, he saw Faibiş coming down the corridor from the locker room, wearing a satisfied smile that seemed like he wanted to reveal a secret but hadn't yet decided whether to do so.

"Hello, my friend. Got any good news?"

"No, none at all."

"Your eyes look different today. Listen, I think I know who assaulted Anişoara the other day..."

"I'm listening."

"I believe it was Engineer Decu," Dan whispered. "I went to the militia and spoke with the officer investigating the case."

"I don't know. I think it was his brother. Only that brute could have done it!"

"Either way, I have my reasons to believe it was him. How could a lathe worker have taken Anişoara there, hmm?"

"I don't know. We'll see," Faibiş said and walked away.

Back at his desk, Dan picked up the phone and dialed a number. At the infirmary, while passing by the nurse's desk, he had copied the internal number, and now he decided to try to get some information about Anișoara's condition. But just then, Engineer Decu stormed into the office. Visibly upset, he picked up his own phone and called the operator:

"Comrade, please call the ambulance and the militia immediately. Someone has been stabbed in the locker room of the mechanical workshop. I don't know... I think he's dead. Who? My brother, Comrade Ion Decu. I didn't find him—a comrade from the afternoon shift, who came to change, did. Please, right away!"

He hung up and rushed out again.

Dan and Comrade Vintilă followed him toward the locker room. They couldn't get in; too many people were gathered in front of the entrance, and only Engineer Decu was allowed to go inside. Comrade Decu was pronounced dead when the ambulance arrived. The same militia officer who had investigated the section days earlier returned to investigate this new case, possibly a revenge killing, following the previous crime. Though the crimes seemed different, it was hard not to find a connection between them. Moreover, the same characters seemed involved, and the common denominator in both cases appeared to be Engineer Decu, whose name had been repeatedly mentioned by the initial victim. Like a few days ago, the workers from the mechanical workshop were once again questioned by the same militia officer, who left no detail of each statement unexamined. The captain wanted to question first the head of the department, but he had asked to accompany his brother in the ambulance, and the officer had agreed, only after the engineer promised to report to the militia the next morning for a statement.

Apparently, none of the people interviewed had any idea who may have committed this crime, except one who seemed more shaken by the events, being a friend of the victim, Comrade Cocoi. Although he had no proof, he suspected that no one else could be responsible for the crimes except Comrade Cristescu, the timekeeper.

"Why do you think Comrade Cristescu was interested in committing these crimes?" asked the officer.

"Out of passion, sir. He found a girl here, beautiful as a flower, and set his sights on her. When things didn't go his way, he went and knocked her out. That's it, comrade, it's passion. With Comrade Decu, just wait and see; he had problems with him, too. He docked his pay. There was a whole scandal about that. See the connection? That's why I believe it's him."

"But how do you know that Comrade Cristescu assaulted the victim?"

"Well, didn't I find her lying on the ground? Wasn't I the

first one to see her, and didn't I call the master there to help the girl? And who went to get the doctor from the infirmary? Wasn't that me, too? That's why I know," Cocoi concluded.

"But I don't understand—you work at a machine; why did you go to the back room?"

"Well, Comrade Anișoara asked me for the key to the room, and she didn't come back to return it. So, I went to check if she was still working or not."

"And when you got there, what did you see?"

"I saw her lying on the ground behind the table, covered in blood."

"Did you look at her? What did she look like?" the officer asked, recalling Master Stoica's description of how he found the girl partially undressed.

"Well, as I said, she was covered in blood."

"And how were her clothes?"

"Also covered in blood."

"Here's the deal. I need you to go to the infirmary for a blood test. Go with the comrade standing next to me!" The captain wrote a note addressed to Doctor Herșcovici, asking him to take a blood sample for analysis, which is necessary to identify the person of interest in connection with Anișoara's sexual assault.

"Why, Comrade Captain, do I need to take a blood test? What did I do wrong?"

"That remains to be seen. Go with the comrade!"

Later that evening at the infirmary, Doctor Herșcovici told Mr. Murguleanu that he would have to admit Anișoara to the psychiatric hospital in Berceni as her psychological condition was not improving. While her physical injuries seemed to be healing, she continued to suffer mentally. Therefore, he had spoken to a doctor, a former classmate who worked at Hospital No. 9, and they would take her there the next morning.

Out in the corridor, Anișoara's father conveyed the news to his wife, Dan, and Faibiș. Dan let Faibiș visit Anișoara before him. Faibiș sat on the edge of her bed, gently stroking her hand, and whispered:

"Comrade Decu has received his punishment. He was found dead. Justice has been served!" He looked into her eyes to see if she understood. He left her with the impression that he had seen a glimmer of light in her eyes.

When it was Dan's turn, he approached her bed cautiously. They examined each other silently, without a word. When he tried to touch her hand, Anișoara pulled it away. A tear rolled down his cheek.

"Why, Anişoara, won't you let me love you?" She turned her gaze away from him. He waited for a moment longer, hoping to catch another glimpse of her, but it never came.

* * *

Several weeks passed, marked by surprising changes in the mechanical workshop following Anişoara's attack and the tragic death of comrade Decu. Two days after the discovery of the body in the locker room, comrade Cocoi, the party secretary of the department, was taken from his workplace by two policemen and imprisoned. A week later, a young engineer replaced Decu, appearing at the office in his place. No one had replaced Anişoara yet, but word spread that she had been allowed to go home under her parents' supervision. Dan, in collaboration with foreman Stoica and the new section head, began timing the execution of certain production tasks setting new work norms.

One day, during the shift change, the personnel department descended upon the men's locker room, gathering all the employees in front of their lockers and instructing them to open and empty them onto the benches beneath each door. A worker with a large metal bin, like those used by street sweepers, passed by each locker while the personnel officers indicated what could be returned to the locker and what should be discarded.

Among those present for this unexpected inspection was

88

Faibiş. The cleaning process seemed slow, and judging by the number of unchecked lockers ahead of him, it could take over an hour. Faibiş approached one of the personnel officers to explain that he needed to return to his workshop to finish his tasks. However, all his arguments were met with a firm and categorical refusal. As the bin drew closer to his locker, Faibiş grew more nervous, sorting and arranging his belongings on the bench and in the locker, his change of clothes, some gloves left over from winter, an umbrella, and other items. The bin was filling up with packages of food scraps, rotten fruit, greasy tools that every section complained were missing from inventory and needed replacing, and even magazines of an obscene nature.

Finally, it was Faibiş's turn. One of the personnel officers approached his locker to look inside. Since the narrow locker didn't allow much light to penetrate, the view was further obstructed by Faibiş, who stood in the way. The officer asked him to step aside, and when he didn't, the officer forcefully made room to inspect the contents. At the bottom of the locker, the officer found a paper bag with a soft object inside. He pulled out a nearly new one-piece coverall, which could be worn over regular clothes. As he unfolded it, a hunting knife fell to the cement floor. Dry bloodstains appeared on the chest, belly, and even the pants of the overall.

"What's this?" the officer asked.

"I slaughtered a pig for an acquaintance," Faibiş replied with a laugh.

"How can you laugh, comrade, when a man was stabbed to death here?"

"It wasn't the same pig."

Two personnel officers grabbed Faibiş by the arms and took him upstairs to their office, along with the overall and the knife. News of Faibiş's arrest spread through the plant like wildfire. No one could understand why Faibiş, and why comrade Decu? They were like two insoluble elements, like oil and water. However, Dan recalled the strange image of Faibiş on the day of the murder when he encountered him in the corridor of the workshop.

After work, Dan went to see Anişoara at her parents' house. He told them what had happened at the plant, and everyone except Anişoara was shaken by the news, deeply moved by the tragedy, and filled with sorrow for their friend and his family, who were likely informed of the horror of this accusation.

Anişoara sat in her room, motionless in an armchair, without saying a word, her gaze fixed on an indeterminate point in the room. She could sit like this for hours, as rigid as a statue and just as silent, despite her parents' attempts to bring her out of this state. Dan sat on a chair against the wall, far from her, wringing his hands as he searched for a way to speak to her without causing her to burst into tears or send him away. After a long period of silence, Dan finally spoke, his voice barely above a whisper, the words hanging in the air, defying the laws of sound:

"You know I would never hurt you."

Anișoara moved her gaze from Dan's hands to the rug stretching across the room toward the door.

"You will never know how much I regret that fate led me to you, into that cursed technical office, only to disrupt your life with my presence."

The girl's eyes now focused on his sorrowful face, from which the words seemed to be drawn with great effort from the depths of his soul.

"It was neither my purpose nor my desire to fall in love with you, but it happened. You came into my life like a miracle when the world seemed to be collapsing around me, and there was no escape for anyone. You separated darkness from light and gave me the love and optimism I had been missing. And now you take them away again."

Tears began to flow from Anișoara's eyes.

"I release you."

Dan looked at her, surprised to hear her speak after so long. He noticed the small cross he had given her shining on her neck, and he gained more courage.

"My dear. My love, you're better now! Let me hold you in my arms; let me kiss you!"

"No! It's not possible anymore! What was is no longer. It's over!" she said, turning her gaze away. "There are many girls who can give you what I can no longer give. Don't waste your time on me."

Dan stood up, wanting to approach Anișoara, but she stopped him by raising her hand. He knelt before her, stretching out his hands as if pleading for a lighter sentence.

"Why, Anișoara, why? We could be so happy, we could start a family, have children, we could—"

Anișoara interrupted him, her voice breaking.

"No, we cannot. I am tainted now!"

"No, you're not tainted. You are holier and purer than all the saints in the world. Don't say such things. When we have children, when you kiss them, you'll realize you're just as innocent and pure as they are."

"I won't have children, and I won't kiss them. Don't you understand? My mouth has been tainted! My body has been tainted. The soul inside me is tainted. I don't want to taint you too! You're free now. Find yourself an unspoiled girl. I don't deserve you anymore!"

Tears welled up in Dan's eyes as he tried to move closer to her knees.

"But Anişoara, don't you understand that I love you? That you are all I have and want in life? Don't push me away, my dear girl; don't punish me for the sins of others!"

"I release you. You must be free! Free!"

After Dan left, the house was enveloped in silence and darkness. Only the autumn wind rustled the leaves in the trees. The sky seemed more opaquer that night, covered by clouds that hid both the moon and the stars. Left alone in her room, Anişoara remained seated in the armchair where she had returned after locking the front door and turning off the remaining lights. She couldn't sleep, feeling her heart break between her love for Dan and the duty she had imposed on herself to save him from a disastrous union. From the moment of the attack in the meeting room, when she had been assaulted by the lathe worker, she knew her dream of becoming Dan's wife was shattered. At that moment, a soulless and inhumane creature had destroyed her life and all her dreams, turning her into something broken. To her, there was no difference between the defilement of the assault and a plague like leprosy. From now on, she no longer had the right to touch him, nor could she allow him to stay.

It was becoming increasingly difficult to resist his desire to hold her, and no argument seemed to make him understand that they could not and should not continue their relationship. She could see how much he suffered, and she pitied the torment she caused him, easily readable on his face. But she suffered just as much, if not more, because she had never stopped loving him as much as before, and at the same time, the cause of their pain was a poison she herself had created, consuming both their hearts. No, he would never abandon her. She knew that! She didn't know what to do to save him. Why must she condemn him to a wasted life, a senseless sacrifice on the altar of a love that had never truly been fulfilled? Why wouldn't he leave her so they could each carry their cross in silence? The cross! She pulled the chain from her neck and brought the small cross to her lips to kiss it, but she hesitated. Gripping it tightly in her fist, she opened the front door and headed to the woodshed.

"He must be free," she told herself.

In the darkness, she found the little bottle that foreman Stoica had given her for the mice, pulled out the cork, and raised it to her lips.

"He must be free."

# Rozica

96

# Rozica

The arrest of Faibiș coincided with Anișoara's last day of life. Her desperate act rendered Faibiș's attempt to bring justice to an unprecedented injustice futile. Whether connected or scattered, these events continued to string together like beads on a thread whose end remained unpredictable. Who would continue to pay the price for the suffering that added up like domino pieces in a line with two open ends and unknown consequences?

Leaving Anișoara's place the night before, Dan walked home, trying to make sense of why she firmly rejected every attempt to get closer to his beloved. He couldn't understand what drove her to behave this way, and her words that night, telling him he was free and should find another girl in her place, seemed like a mere excuse to push him away. Why? What hurt the most was that nobody knew anything. The only tangible outcome was the result of the attack, but the perpetrator, the motive for trying to kill her, and what happened in that room remained unknown. There were rumors that Anișoara had been assaulted, someone had been stabbed by Faibiș because of it, and both Cocoi and apparently engineer Decu had been arrested. But all Dan could learn from Anișoara that night was that she had been soiled. What did she mean by that? Soiled in what way?

After a mostly sleepless night, the next morning, when Dan

entered his office, he stood for a long moment, staring at her empty desk. She used to smile at him from behind it, her joy akin to the warmth of meeting a loved one in the early hours of the day with a promise of a good day ahead. Now, looking at the empty spot, he wondered how long it would be before Anișoara regained her strength and returned to this office, which missed her like the sky misses the sun behind the clouds. At around ten in the morning, the secretary of the Personnel Department came to inform him that he needed to go urgently to Comrade Murguleanu's house.

"But what happened?" Dan asked.

"I don't know. All I know is that the boss told his driver to take you there. He said it was urgent. The car is waiting for you in front of the factory."

On the street, in front of Anișoara's house, two cars were parked, and a guard stood watch at the gate. The main door of the house was wide open, and the girl's mother, her head wrapped in a black scarf, was crying, holding a handkerchief to her mouth to wipe away her tears. She was hunched on a chair, staring at the table where her elbows rested. Next to her, an elderly priest with a graying beard was trying to console her. Inside Anișoara's room stood a militia captain, several others, and her father beside the nightstand where the girl lay on the bed. She appeared to be sleeping, oblivious to the commotion around her. Dan still couldn't grasp what was happening. When the captain saw him, he asked:

"Comrade Cristescu, were you here last night?"

"Yes."

"Was anyone else here when you spoke with Comrade Murguleanu?"

"No. Just the two of us."

"Did you give her anything to eat or drink?"

"No. Nothing."

"Did you go with her to the storage room in the yard?"

"No, Comrade Captain. After speaking with Anişoara's parents, I talked to her here, in this room."

"Did you argue? What did you talk about?"

"We never argued. She told me she was letting me go, that I should find another girl because she could no longer be what she had wanted for me. I tried to encourage her, but she wouldn't listen and kept saying I was free."

"What do you know about this bottle?"

"Nothing. What's with it?"

"It seems she drank its contents. It's poison."

Dan felt his knees weaken.

"Anişoara is dead?"

"Yes. You were the last person to be in contact with her. I'll have to detain you until the investigation is complete."

**Monday, October 15**

When she woke up that morning, Mrs. Murguleanu tiptoed to the door of Anişoara's bedroom to make sure the girl was still asleep. So as not to wake her, she told her husband to keep quiet and then went outside to light the fire in the kitchen and prepare breakfast. She was relieved that Anişoara was home again, that she could once more admire her face, now free of bandages, and with God's help, all their worries would pass. Meanwhile, her husband quietly slipped out of the house and went to the woodshed to fetch more firewood for the day. He found it strange that the door was open, but when he stepped inside, he saw his daughter lying on her side near the entrance.

"Anişoara, what's wrong?" he shouted, but receiving no answer, he knelt beside her. She was cold. He lifted her from the ground, cradled her in his arms, sobbing, and with a voice choked by tears, he pleaded with the heavens:

"Oh, Lord Christ, why do you punish me? If you knew you'd take her from me, why didn't you take her when that villain tried to kill her? Why, Lord, did you let her suffer after all the pain we all endured since then? Why, Lord, when she had done nothing wrong?"

He laid her back down and went to tell his wife, but he couldn't say a word and collapsed onto a chair. At her alarmed question, all he could do was raise his arm, pointing toward the woodshed, while continuing to cry. When his wife rushed out to see what had happened, Mr. Murguleanu followed her, ready to support her. Kneeling beside Anişoara's body, they wept inconsolably for a time before his wife rose to fetch a candle from the house and place it at their daughters' head. They caressed her forehead and hair between kisses, just as they had when she was a child. They decided they had to bring her into the house to her soft, warm bed. As they lifted her, a small bottle fell from her hand, while in the other, Anişoara still tightly clutched a silver crucifix.

"Go, Gică, to the church and ask Father to come and say a prayer!"

Father Niculae, who had baptized her at birth, upon hearing of Anişoara's death, asked if Mr. Murguleanu had notified the police. When he learned that they hadn't, he went to the phone to report the death himself and then headed to the girl's house.

**Thursday, October 18th**

Anişoara's funeral took place days later at the local cemetery in Băneasa, on the outskirts of Bucharest, where her grandfather, Mr. Murguleanu, had built a family tomb. It was a cold, sorrowful autumn day, matching the hearts of those who accompanied her on her final journey. With red eyes from tears and sobs, the women who had watched Anişoara grow walked in the procession, supported by those around them, following the hearse. Behind them were family, friends, neighbors, and many colleagues from the plant, including Master Stoica, Mr. Vintilă, and Dan. Father Niculae and the church deacon led the procession with heavy hearts, burdened by the guilt of officiating at the funeral of a suicide victim, a grave sin in their faith, but they couldn't let her leave this world without a Christian prayer. Master Stoica was no less troubled. Upon hearing that Anişoara had poisoned herself, he was overwhelmed with remorse and contacted the militia captain leading the investigation to confess his part in the matter. Dan, meanwhile, was both present and absent. He walked behind the procession but was oblivious of what was happening around him. Inside, Anişoara's face loomed larger and more serious than in life, reminding him again and again: "I told you I'd set you free. Now you are free, and you can't oppose it anymore!"

"Yes. I cannot oppose you anymore, dear Anişoara," Dan said in his mind, as if in dialogue with her image, which he saw vividly in his mind's eye. "But I can't forgive myself for being the reason you gave up on life. In the eyes of God, I remain forever guilty, and nothing can wash away the blood of your sacrifice. You didn't free me; you condemned me. I am stained with your blood, or, as you put it, I am soiled. You are no more, but I must carry this burden."

Lost in these thoughts, Dan watched the procession reach the cemetery, the entire religious ceremony, the lowering of the coffin into the family tomb, and the return to Anişoara's house. There, the women had laid out a meal around which Father Niculae, the deacon, and the other funeral attendees gathered. Trays of food were brought from the kitchen, and the brandy and wine loosened tongues, changing the somber mood of the procession walk into something livelier. Dan, however, rose from the table, took a bottle of ţuica brandy and a glass, and stepped outside, where a bench next to the kitchen window was free. Here, solitude suited him better. After a while, Mr. Murguleanu, Anişoara's father, joined him. "Would you like something to eat?" Dan shook his head, signaling a not answer. A long silence followed. Dan finished his first glass of ţuica and poured another. Mr. Murguleanu stared into the distance over the fence where a crow appeared, cawing. He then placed a hand on Dan's shoulder:

"You are like a son to us. Now we have no one closer. Come visit us when you can. In our home, you are always welcome." Choked with emotion, he wiped away a tear, stood up, and left.

Dan emptied his glass, placed the bottle on the kitchen window ledge, and left as well. He took the tram from the square in front of the plant, sat on a bench in the second-class carriage, and fell asleep. When he awoke, the tram was crossing Izvor Bridge, under which the Dâmbovița River flowed peacefully. He got off at the stop after Uranus on Splaiul Independenței street. Outside, it had started to drizzle, and Dan turned up the collar on his coat, continuing to walk upstream along the river without paying much attention. The light rain and darkened sky soothed him; they matched the cloudiness and tears of his soul. With his hands deep in his pockets, he trudged along the deserted sidewalks of the Dâmbovița's embankment, seeing nothing but the wet pavement beneath his feet. He passed Elefterie Bridge, then Grozăvești Bridge, and as he continued toward the dam, he came upon an open restaurant. He realized he was wet, cold, and hungry. He went inside.

The place was crowded, mostly with men who seemed well acquainted with each other. They occupied several tables, talking loudly and raising their glasses in toast. A man with a violin on his shoulder, accompanied by another with a portable dulcimer hanging around his neck, moved between the tables, playing "M-a făcut mama oltean" (a popular folk song). It appeared to be payday at the nearby metallurgical plant, and this made Dan glimpse a new possibility:

"This plant is much closer to home. I can't work there anymore now that she's gone. I must transfer here."

## Friday, October 19th

The next morning, Dan didn't go to work. He felt dizzy and thought he had a fever because, during the night, he dreamt he was floating like a leaf in the air while strange shapes spun continuously before his eyes. Whenever he had visions like this, he knew he had a fever. But now he got out of bed and went into the kitchen, where his aunt had made a fire and had a pot boiling on the stove. The coat he had worn the previous evening lay crumpled on a chair, still wet. Dan realized that if he wanted to go anywhere that day, he would need to iron it, as it was unwearable otherwise. He went to fetch his aunt's iron, filled it with embers from the stove, added a few more coals from the winter supply, and placed it outside on the cement step to heat up. In the meantime, his aunt warmed some milk for him in a small pot while spreading marmalade on a slice of bread. Dan sat down at the table.

"I'm going to the plant near the dam to look for work. I want to change jobs."

"It's a shame, dear. You were doing so well at the plant there."

"I can't go back to that office. It's like a magnetic force will pull me into the darkness of the tomb where she lies. It's not that I want to forget her, but I can't relive this tragedy every minute of the day."

"All right, Dan, do what you think is best," his aunt relented.

At around ten in the morning, Dan left the house. It was a fresh day with clear skies and gentle sunlight. He walked through the park near Regie, in a valley that had been filled with new houses in recent years while the new blocks of the student district had risen. Crossing the footbridge over the river, he entered the gatekeeper's hut at the entrance to the plant.

"Good day. I'd like to speak with the factory's Party secretary if possible."

"Who are you, and what's this about?"

"My name is Daniel Cristescu, and it's a personal matter."

The gatekeeper called on the phone and began filling out a slip from a pre-printed pad. "Bring this back with the Party secretary's signature."

A wide gravel path opened before the gate, with buildings on either side, separated by narrow streets. The most imposing structure was the administrative building in front of the gatekeeper's hut, behind which stood many enormous halls with zigzagging roofs and metal-framed, tilting windows.

The Party organization building was on the left, behind the clinic. A secretary led Dan to Comrade Roşca, the Party secretary. A man of average height with partially gray hair and wearing a blue work coat sat behind a desk adorned with a telephone, a lamp, a few newspapers, and some papers. When Dan was introduced, Comrade Roșca stood up.

"Have a seat. How can I help you?" he asked after shaking Dan's hand.

"I'm a technician, a work norms planner. I work in the Technical Department of the Herăstrău Plant, but my fiancée, who worked in the same office, was assaulted by a brute at work, and yesterday I buried her. I can't work there anymore. Please help me transfer here."

"Have you spoken to your colleagues at the Plant? Will they release you to come here?"

"Not yet. I came to you first. I don't know how they will respond. Please understand, it is absolutely impossible for me to step foot in that office again."

"I understand. They might offer you a position in a different department. Go there and see what they say. When you leave here, give my secretary an employment application, and we'll see what we can do. Good luck!" said the secretary, shaking Dan's hand as he bid him farewell.

## Saturday, October 20th

Comrade Fazekaş listened quietly to everything Dan said:

"Comrade Cristescu, I don't have anyone to replace you there right now. I understand, and I want to help you, but I need time to find someone suitable for your position. Do you understand? Until I find someone, I can't let you go."

"No, Comrade Fazekaş. I can't go back there. You're asking more of me than I can handle. Comrade Engineer and master Stoica can manage for a short while without me, and you have plenty of comrades here at the plant who can take my place. Please, let me go."

The woman in front of Dan remained thoughtful, watching his face, which had inexplicably matured in such a short time. She felt pity for him. She was caught between her own challenges and this young man, consumed by a tragedy that everyone in this busy community had witnessed but none as deeply as he had. She decided to help him.

"I have a friend at the Metallurgical Plant, Engineer Istrate, whom I've stayed in touch with. I'll call her today and recommend you. Come back in an hour to pick up your transfer."

Dan couldn't believe that Comrade Fazekaş had agreed to let him go.

"I'm so grateful, Comrade Fazekaş. You have a heart of gold, and you understand how hard it was for me to make this request. Thank you!"

"Alright, alright. Good luck!"

**Monday, October 22nd**

Dan started his new job on Monday morning, though not as a work-norms technician. Comrade Istrate was the head of the specific material consumption group and needed a technician. The group located in the prototype area of the factory is part of the large rooms assigned to the Technical Service. Several departments functioned there: designing and improving new products, the tooling service, the technological service, and documentation copying. Within the technological service there were various groups of technicians, some elaborating the technological process, others setting time standards for execution, and finally, the specific consumption team led by Comrade Corina Istrate. Many desks lined up the room, with the specific material consumption section occupying the corner area near the entrance door, with six large desks and a few metal cabinets for documents. Comrade Engineer Istrate had a desk by the wall next to the door, giving her the ability to monitor not only her group but also the entire room.

Entering for the first time, Dan noticed that there were only two women in the entire room, one of whom, wearing an orange coat, sat at the desk behind the door. Dan went straight to her:

"Excuse me, are you Engineer Istrate?"

"Yes, that's me. How can I help you?"

"My name is Daniel Cristescu. Comrade Fazekaș from the Herăstrău Plant said she spoke with you."

"Yes. Please, take a seat. In fact, the desk where you're sitting now will be yours. So... I've been told you're a technician. Do you know how to read a technical drawing?"

"Of course," Dan replied.

"Look here, see this part?" she continued, unfolding a drawing of a metal object with bent edges. "Can you tell me what kind of material you'd need to make it and what dimensions it should have?"

Dan mentally calculated the width of the bent edges, added to the length between them, and gave her the overall unfolded dimension. The engineer seemed satisfied.

"Good... but could you tell me what material and roughly how much of it?"

"Well, it needs to be decarburized sheet metal, 2 millimeter thick, multiplied by the unfolded length and width of the part. I just can't remember the specific weight of steel..."

"Approximately 8 kilograms per cubic decimeter. That's right... have you ever worked with a slide rule?"

"No," Dan admitted. "I haven't had the chance yet."

"Well, Comrade Mănoiu will show you how, but not right now. For now, go to Personnel and complete your hiring paperwork. I assume you have a transfer letter from the plant. Take it there. When you're done, come back, and we'll see what else we need to do. Alright... let me introduce you to your colleagues. This here is Comrade Bărbulescu..."

Engineer Istrate's desk was positioned perpendicular to Comrade Bărbulescu's. He was a tall man with glasses and graying hair, dressed in a blue coat like most of the technicians in the room. His desk was aligned with that of Comrade Mănoiu, a younger woman with a pleasant appearance, whom the supervisor tasked with teaching Dan how to use the slide rule. Dan's desk was parallel to Engineer Istrate's, facing Comrade Sorin Petrescu, and behind him was Comrade Nestorescu's desk.

After the introductions, Dan headed to Personnel, feeling pleased that, starting today, a new chapter in his life had begun.

**Monday, October 29th**

Soon, Dan began to acclimate to the atmosphere in the large room, where over twenty people worked, spread across different teams. They all knew each other, indulging in-jokes and playful antics that gave the place a youthful air, like a high school classroom. Most of them were under thirty, many unmarried, and their daily preoccupation seemed to be debating the standings of football teams from Serie A, predicting the outcomes of upcoming matches. In Dan's group, the "specific consumption of materials" team, comrade Istrate, an imposing blonde woman in her forties, always dressed in elegant suits, maintained a calculated distance from the rest of the group, which bolstered her authority. Comrade Bărbulescu, the group's senior member, was a former career officer with a law degree. He had a gentle demeanor, wasn't a party member, but held decisive sway over the drafting of material consumption standards. Comrade Mănoiu was the opposite in every way to her female boss being brunette, younger, vivacious and constantly competing with her superior in elegance. Her lab coat, always unbuttoned, was made of silky black material, more akin to a judge's robe than work attire. Both women were married and childless, and their husbands held important positions of responsibility in the army or security.

Dan's desk faced Sorin Petrescu, whom he initially struggled to understand until he discovered that Sorin was deaf-mute. Learning of the immense effort Sorin made to grasp conversations and respond, often with forced sounds, Dan developed a deep respect for him. Sorin was from a wealthy family, but his father, a former lawyer, had been murdered by robbers after the war. Comrade Nestorescu, another colleague, was a former security officer who had been expelled in one of the early purges from the Ministry of Internal Affairs, likely for lacking the necessary ruthlessness. He was in a long-term relationship with a woman everyone called "Pisicuța" (Kitty), who accompanied him on all outings with colleagues.

Dan's first task was to calculate material consumption for a subassembly from a new project. Every part made from sheet metal, steel, cast iron, wood, or other materials, including the number of welding electrodes, needed to be tabulated on individual sheets, specifying the quantities for each grade, dimension, and profile. Even standardized parts like screws, nuts, and washers required their own consumption sheets in case they needed to be manufactured in-house. Calculating the raw material quantities finally made Dan understand why he had been asked if he knew how to use a slide rule. With a few swift movements of the ruler and cursor, he could calculate the necessary material. On his first day, he received a worn-out slide rule from the Soviet Union, its markings nearly erased. Comrade Mănoiu invited him to bring his chair next to hers, explaining how to use it. These lessons, exercises, and approximation rules spanned several extended sessions, allowing them to talk about personal matters and share information about their lives.

As they worked closely together, Dan found himself unavoidably aware of Mănoiu's proximity, her breath brushing his face, and at times, her knee would accidentally graze his leg under the table. From her, Dan learned that Istrate, despite her airs and claims of beauty, was just a simple countrywoman. Beneath layers of makeup, you could see the sunburnt skin where her headscarf couldn't protect her from the sun. Mănoiu also confided that everyone knew comrade Nestorescu was a crook, a heavy drinker who accepted bribes, which was why he had been kicked out of the Ministry of Internal Affairs, where her husband is one of the directors

Dan's work was occasionally interrupted by tasks from his boss, such as delivering a letter or material for typing to the service's secretary. The secretary, comrade Rosner, worked in the adjacent hall at the S.D.V. (Tools and Devices) section. She was nearing retirement age, a petite woman with dyed black hair that revealed patches of scalp. She wore glasses and painted her lips in a garish shade of red. Surprisingly, she was fast on her typewriter, and she could talk about various topics while typing flawlessly. However, she had many enemies because of her sharp tongue, as she made cutting remarks about anyone nearby. When Dan approached her, she barely glanced at him before saying:

"Are you comrade Cristescu, the new guy? Tell me, don't you use deodorant?"

"No. Why?"

"Because you're sweating, and I can smell it. Go to a pharmacy and buy one. It's not expensive."

Dan was stunned. A draftswoman nearby, working on a drawing, turned to look at him, smiling. He caught the glance of the blonde-haired girl and blushed.

**Thursday, November 1st**

Comrade Bărbulescu had been extremely busy lately, preparing a report of objections to the Ministry regarding next year's consumption standards, which had been cut by 10% from the factory's already reduced requests. He and comrade Istrate had exchanged many words, often disagreeing, as he justified his points in the report. Istrate, though she spoke in a calm voice, showed her disapproval through the redness in her face:

"Yes, but you won't be the one, comrade Bărbulescu, to support these numbers at the Ministry. I will. You don't know the kind of pressure they apply, and you can't even have a discussion with them... all they do is pass down orders from above."

"I know one thing: without materials, we can't meet production! Does anyone think machines can be made with magic? Let anyone come and tell me what I can eliminate from a machine, and I'll do it. That's the limit!"

Though new to the job, Dan had already seen how the factory's products were being deliberately compromised by so-called innovations meant to reduce material consumption. The innovators were rewarded with a 15% salary bonus based on the savings they achieved. For instance, one part, shaped like a parallelogram with a diagonal over a meter long, was originally made from a sheet of metal measuring 1 meter by 2 meters. The innovator suggested cutting it into three smaller pieces, which saved material but weakened the structural integrity of the product, making it prone to accidents. These patchwork machines were shoddy, and cases like this soon became widespread.

One day after work, Dan decided to take a reconnaissance walk through the factory. He moved from hall to hall, stopping to watch unfamiliar machines in action, observing the steel casting process, and eventually reached the forging workshop. Here, red-hot steel bars were forged into different shapes and sizes under the blows of automated friction-powered hammers. It was late, but his tour wasn't over yet. Behind the casting and forging hall ran a railway line, serviced by a platform for loading and unloading train cars. Two overhead cranes moved on tracks high above, handling raw materials or finished products for distribution across the country. At the edge of this platform were several guillotines used to cut sheets of metal according to plans drawn by the consumption technicians. Some of these guillotines were used for cutting thick sheets. The cut-off pieces were stored on rolling platforms and transported to the preparation section. Powerful floodlights illuminated the exposed platform, subject to all weather conditions.

That evening, Ștefan, a young man from a nearby village who commuted daily by train, was on duty. Dan stopped chatting with him:

"How's it going, comrade Ștefan? Was your last proposal for innovation on the galvanized sheet metal approved?"

"I'm not sure yet. You see, I've been on the evening shift and haven't had the chance to come in early and talk to the comrades. I'll check next week when I'm on the morning shift. But you know what I was thinking? Look at all these materials. They're scraps we can't use for any of our products. It felt wrong to load them up as waste for re-melting, so I kept them here. We can't use them, but others would pay anything to get them. Couldn't we sell them?"

Dan glanced at the pile of materials gathered at the edge of the platform—strips of metal in various sizes and numerous leftover steel bars and pipes. The idea seemed excellent.

"Haven't you spoken to anyone about this?"

"No. No one comes here to talk to us."

"I'll look into it and let you know. Congratulations! I think it's a fantastic idea."

**Friday, November 2nd**

The next morning, Dan turned to Comrade Istrate to report what he had discussed with Comrade Ștefan. Comrade Bărbulescu also listened closely to what Dan had to say. The engineer, already somewhat surprised, watched Bărbulescu's reaction. He took his time to share his thoughts, his silence adding weight to the value of Dan's information. Eventually, Comrade Bărbulescu began to speak:

"Indeed, many enterprises and cooperatives could benefit from these materials. Comrade Ștefan's proposal is valuable, but legally, I don't believe there's a defined way for us to sell our excess materials. Where could we advertise that we have materials available? In Informația Bucureștiului paper? Who sets the price— you, me, or him? And then, who receives the money, and in what form? These are issues we cannot decide on our own. First, the system in which this proposal can be implemented needs to be established."

Everyone remained deep in thought, pondering these questions. In the end, it was again Comrade Bărbulescu who proposed a course of action:

"I believe, Comrade Istrate, that it would be best for you to go with Comrade Cristescu to see exactly what we're dealing with. After that, a detailed inventory needs to be made—profiles, lengths, quantities, and even dimensional sketches for the sheet metal scraps. Once that's done, you'll take these lists to the director and report Comrade Ştefan's proposal."

Again, this plan seemed reasonable. The engineer looked at Dan.

"Shall we go there now?"

Dan grabbed a notepad, a caliper, and a tape measurement from his drawer, then left the office with his superior. On their way, she said:

"Tomorrow, I want to submit the report to the ministry about next year's material consumption. I'd like you to accompany me so I can introduce you to the comrades there, and in the future, you can deliver our reports. We'll leave around nine in the morning. Does that work for you?"

"Of course. Whatever you think is best."

They arrived at the concrete platform where the guillotines were installed. Two overhead cranes were busy unloading open railway cars. A tractor was pulling a stock of thick sheet metal from a railcar installed on a wooden sled. The pile of scrap material saved by Comrade Ştefan was at the edge of the platform, and it represented a substantial amount. The engineer looked at the materials haphazardly scattered on the ground and asked Dan:

"Will you stay here to do an inventory of these materials?"

"Yes, but I'll need someone to help me move them."

The engineer went off to find the dock supervisor for assistance. Dan began the task of taking inventory.

**Saturday, November 3rd**

The next morning, Comrade Istrate and Dan took the tram from the factory to the ministry. They sat quietly next to each other on a first-class bench—she in an elegant gabardine coat, and he in his navy pinstriped suit, bought with ration points. They got off at the Izvor bridge and cut their way through Cişmigiu Park, heading towards the Victoriei Way. At the ministry, Comrade Istrate entered a few offices accompanied by Dan, introduced him to the staff, and submitted the report, stapled in a folder, to the head of the department. She argued:

"The plant cannot meet next year's production targets without the materials we've requested. We've already reduced consumption by more than 10% compared to this year! We can't reduce any further!"

"Comrade Istrate. We've committed to the Central Committee and the working class to reduce material consumption, and you're here to tell me that it can't be done? Is that even possible? Your attitude, Comrade Istrate, is embarrassing. Understand this!

Comrade Minister cannot allow your refusal!"

"Comrade Haralambie, I invite you to come to the plant and show me where we can cut any more material. Not from your comfortable office. Come to the plant and show me that it's possible! That's all I have to say. Here's the report with all the evidence that our request is justified. Review it and give us an answer. Goodbye!"

The department head wanted to say more, but it was too late. Comrade Istrate and Dan left the office. On their way back, she was still fuming.

"Can you believe that idiot telling me he's embarrassed for me? Excuse my language, but I'd tell him to shove it where the sun doesn't shine!"

They were walking back toward Cișmigiu Park when she stopped.

"You know what? I have some books to buy at the Cartea Românească library. Let's not go back to the factory today; I'm too irritated. Stay with me, maybe we can watch a film on the boulevard. What do you think?"

Dan nodded slightly. When they reached the front of the Military Circle, she gently tugged him across the street to Capșa confectionery. She ordered two Joffre cakes and coffee, and they sat down at a table.

"My husband's been away for a few days. There's trouble with the students in Timisoara. They've revolted. No one knows how it will end. It doesn't smell good," she said, worried.

"I'm surprised. I haven't read anything about that in România Liberă paper. No mention on the radio either..."

"No, of course not. These things are kept secret. They don't want to feed our enemies with news like this. Understand? Just like they're not saying much about what's happening in Hungary lately. It's bloody bad over there."

A young waitress brought their coffee, glasses of water, and the cakes. Dan reached into his jacket to pay, but the engineer stopped him, pulling a twenty-lei note from her purse. The bookstore was across the street, but she changed her mind.

"I heard Romeo and Juliet is a good movie. Let's see if it's playing now at the matinee."

They strolled down the boulevard toward Cişmigiu. They stopped in the lobby of the Trianon cinema, where the film was still showing. They found seats in the back of the dark theater and sat down. The movie, in color, featured the famous dancer Galina Ulanova, with music by Sergei Prokofiev. Dan, who had never seen a ballet, was mesmerized by the passionate dance of the protagonists, their dramatic love scenes, and the spirit of sacrifice, which brought back memories of his own tragic love with Anişoara, and the warmth of the music softened his heart. During these moments of deep emotional turmoil, Comrade Istrate shifted into her seat, trying to lean down to pick up something from the floor, but the space was too cramped. She asked Dan to retrieve her fallen handkerchief. In the dark, it was hard to see, and the engineer hiked up her skirt over her knees, parting her legs. Holding onto the armrest, he bent forward, and Dan had no choice but to lean across her lap to reach the handkerchief trapped under her seat. As he lifted it, when he tried to pull his hand back, Comrade Istrate closed her knees, trapping his hand between her thighs inside her skirt, where the soft touch of silk always creates an enticing space.

When the film ended and the lights came on, she said:

"Let's go. I've seen enough."

Once they exited through the theater's back door into the back street, she took Dan by the arm.

"Tell me, where do you live?"

Dan explained that he lived with his aunt in a small house in Crângaşi.

"It doesn't matter," she said. "Come, let me show you where I live."

She lived in an old house in the Cotroceni neighborhood. As they neared the house, she asked Dan to walk behind her and not speak, as if they didn't know each other. The entrance had two doors, and she unlocked the one on the left. She left the door slightly ajar behind her, and he slipped inside. A small hallway with several doors led into a large room with a high ceiling, windows facing the street on one side, and elegant, classic furniture. A wide couch, two comfortable armchairs, a desk, a bookshelf full of books, and a fireplace on the wall opposite the windows gave the room a distinguished, modern feel like in the movies. She told him to turn on the radio or television and said she'd be back shortly. Dan didn't want to touch anything, so he sat on the couch, wondering how to leave quickly.

After a few minutes, she returned, dressed in a silk robe, carrying a tray with a bottle of wine, two glasses, and a plate of sliced cake, which she placed on the coffee table in front of the couch. Pouring the wine, she handed a glass to Dan.

"To your health!" she said, clinking her glass with his as she sat down in one of the armchairs. "Now, here's what I want to tell you. I've noticed that Comrade Mănoiu fills your head with her stories. You have no idea what she's really like. She has a good husband who allows her too much freedom. Before I came to the plant, there was a young engineer at my place. She twisted his mind so much that the poor man had to divorce his wife because of her.

Her husband, Comrade Mănoiu, a powerful man, wanted to throw the poor guy out of the job like a dog with a tin can tied to his tail. In the end, he relented. So be careful!"

"I had no idea," Dan replied.

"Of course. I understand that women, even married ones, like all people, go through periods of loneliness, dissatisfaction, and even depression. They also, like drowning people, need a lifesaver, someone close to offer them a bit of understanding and comfort. Do you understand? To be honest, I don't condemn her for needing a little intimacy outside of her marriage. What I condemn is her disloyalty, the way she gossips everywhere, and how dangerous she can be. Do you understand what I'm saying?" Dan nodded in agreement. "So, what do I want to say? I myself am going through one of these moments. I realize I'm getting older and that I've lived half my life. I've accomplished what I've accomplished, but I haven't had time to live. I've been, in a way, my own worst enemy: work, study, obligations, but nothing for me. I didn't even have the chance to have a child of my own. My husband, twenty years older than me, took me into his house like a doll, but he spent all day with others. When he comes home, my duty is to serve him as an orderly, and that's it. I have never known love, I have never loved anyone, and I don't want to continue living like this. I know you're much younger than me, and I don't want to be a burden to you. But from the first day, I've seen in your eyes that you are a special man, that

I could trust your loyalty, and I ask for nothing more than a little warmth of soul. What do you say? Can you help me? Will you be my friend?"

Dan, to be closer, leaned his elbows on his knees, lifting a sad gaze toward her:

"I left my previous plant to forget a sad love that ended with the death of my beloved girl I wanted to marry. She was buried the week before I arrived at the Factory. At that time, I said I would never care about another love, and I think I feel the same today. I don't know if I'm capable of loving again after the tragedy I went through."

His boss rose from her armchair and came closer, wrapping her arms around his shoulders:

"Don't say that, Dan, you don't know. I was complaining about my foolish suffering when you're the one who needs comfort. Lay your head on my shoulder, Dan, let me hold you. I will be your mother and sister if you don't have one. Stay with me, please, and don't torment yourself anymore. There you go…"

**Monday, November 5th**

Sorin, Dan's colleague who sat at the desk in front of his, was staring over his shoulder at the back wall or something else with a statue-like, motionless gaze. Dan tried to get his attention, but

Sorin signaled for him to wait. Curious, Dan turned his head to see what Sorin was looking at. Through the window on the back wall behind comrade Istrate, the communist party secretary, comrade Rosca, was engaged in a conversation with the chief engineer, Budău. Soon, both entered the office. Following them, the people from the adjacent offices, the designers, technicians, clerks, and even those preparing the documentation filled all the available spaces between the desks in the room. Beside Dan's chair, comrade Rosner, the short and stocky typist, appeared. Dan stood up and gave her his seat. Behind the typist was the blonde girl he saw near the secretary working at the drawing board. When he saw her, Dan smiled and let her pass to take his spot, where she had a better view. The girl thanked him. Once everyone had gathered, engineer Budău gave the floor to comrade Roşca, who had an important announcement to make:

"Comrades," began the party secretary, "I don't know to what extent you've been informed about the events taking place in the neighboring country, Hungary, and especially in the capital, Budapest. It has come to our attention that malicious rumors, which have nothing to do with the truth, are being spread by those seeking to undermine our democratic regime. They misinformed the working class with lies, claiming that a popular revolution had broken out in the neighboring country. It is true that certain hostile elements have infiltrated with the intent to incite the masses. Even in our country, in Timisoara, a few instigators were found among the students trying to sow unrest at the university, but the vigilance of the working class dealt with them, isolating them, and now they struggle in vain, trying to escape the people's rightful wrath, which seeks fair justice for their actions. Therefore, we, the Romanian people, in full solidarity with the Hungarian people, strongly condemn all failed attempts by dying imperialism to return us to the life of slavery we had before the liberation of our countries by the glorious Soviet army. We will not admit it, and we will not allow anyone to try to hinder our determined drive to build victorious socialism and maintain national freedom and independence. This is why we have gathered here today because we must remain vigilant, comrades. We must not listen to or be lured by the tools of the class enemy, who, at any cost and in any form, try to stop us on our path. That's all I have to say. Thank you."

After everyone returned to their places, Sorin leaned closer to Dan, speaking quietly:

"That's not what they were discussing in the hallway before the meeting."

"How do you know what they were discussing? You didn't hear them, did you?"

"I hear with my eyes, you fool! They said the revolt in Hungary was still going on, and the Russians brought in tanks against the demonstrators. There are thousands of dead, and Hungarians are fleeing the country in mass. It seems like it's not over yet. They're afraid it might happen here, too."

"Are you sure that's what they were talking about?" Sorin confirmed, leaning back in his chair, watching Dan's reaction. Dan sat back down as well. Curious, comrade Mănoiu glanced at Dan, questioning him with her eyes about what had been said, but cautiously, he responded only with a shrug.

After what he had heard from comrade Istrate, Dan became a bit suspicious of what he had discussed with this woman. For two days, his relations with the boss had become somewhat tense. Afraid of arousing suspicion that there might be something between them, they began to avoid direct contact. The day before, comrade Bărbulescu answered the group's only phone on the boss's desk while she was not there and afterward handed the receiver to Dan. It was her, Crina Istrate, the head of the group, asking for some details about a specific material quantity for the supply department. But in reality, she wanted to ask if he would like to accompany her on Sunday morning to the concert at the Romanian Athenaeum. Dan looked through the documents, provided the answer about the consumption, and confirmed that he would like to attend the concert.

Dan had never had an experience with a woman so sure of herself, knowing exactly what she wanted and yet giving the impression that the initiative belonged to the other person. In all his previous relationships, he had been the one initiating, and the victory belonged solely to him. But things unfolded differently this time. After the conversation in Crina's living room, she came closer, gently wrapping her arms around his shoulders, caressing him tenderly after hearing about his past tragedy. In response, Dan also wrapped his arms around her like a spineless creature in need of support. As he embraced her, he realized that beneath Crina's silk robe, she wore nothing at all. He remembered the conversation with Anişoara at the beach when he had said he didn't know how he would react in front of a naked woman. Overcome by an uncontrollable impulse to be sure, he tugged at the opening of her robe, and before his eyes appeared a lively and full-of-life Eve. Not surprised at all, she looked into his eyes with desire and allowed herself to be laid down on the couch as his hands explored every inch of her body. With a flood of passionate kisses, the exploration continued inward.

**Tuesday, November 6th**

The next day, before lunch, comrade Mănoiu bombarded comrade Bărbulescu with questions about his first marriage. It must have been several years ago because now, with his second wife, they had a school-aged daughter. Comrade Bărbulescu didn't seem embarrassed by the opportunity to tell a story, as he did so with great skill and an unfailing smile on his lips. Whenever they had a bit of free time for storytelling, each of them, including engineer Istrate, would let their pencils rest on the pages of their unfinished work and listen from their desks, except for comrade Nestorescu, who would bring his chair closer to be able to hear better.

"When I returned from the front in 1945," began comrade Bărbulescu, "I was fed up with the army and my officer's career. Six years of war, fighting, and death at every turn were enough for me. I enrolled in law school, but after so many years of war without touching a book, I had a lot to catch up on to keep up with my colleagues. I was still living at the garrison because my parents were in the countryside, and I couldn't find a quiet corner in that military environment to study. That's when I resigned from the army, found a place to rent, and lived off my earnings as a tutor. And what can I tell you? My landlord had a daughter. That's the whole story," he finished with a smile.

"No way, comrade Bărbulescu, you can't leave us hanging like that. "Was it a passionate love, like in the movies?" questioned comrade Mănoiu relentlessly.

"Well, now, it wasn't like what you're imagining. The girl was also a student studying philology. She used to write poems, and she would bring them to me to read. She was romantic and wrote about love, but she didn't really know what love was. It was hard not to love a girl like her, young, beautiful, and intelligent. Her parents didn't quite understand her writing, and they were unhappy that she hadn't chosen a more suitable profession for a girl, like becoming a teacher, a doctor, or something else. That's why she came to me, valuing my opinions. I liked talking to her; we were friends, and her parents were happier to let her go out with me rather than other men they didn't know. But in my uncertain situation, I couldn't risk getting into a serious relationship. Until one day when Jeni, that was her name, forced me to tell her whether or not I loved her and what my intentions were. Caught by surprise, I didn't know what to say to her. She was waiting for me to confess my feelings, and I didn't know whether it was time to do so or not. Until then, I had acted like a friend to her. I treated her as a colleague I respected, with whom I could discuss any subject without attachment or hidden meanings. Now, though, I didn't know what to do.

'We're friends,' I told her. 'If I didn't care for you, would I have stayed by your side all this time? Would we have studied together, and would I have gone with you everywhere? Have you ever seen me with anyone else? Isn't that enough for you?'

'Enough?' Jeni burst out, 'What are we here, in a pharmacy? Measuring things by gram? Now we're friends, and I'm wasting my time with you, but when you feel like it, you will pick up your hat and leave? Of course, it's not enough! I want to know what your intentions are!'

'I have no intentions,' I told her, irritated. 'I'm not able to have intentions. When God wills it, and I get my degree, then we can talk. That's all I can say.'

She left, slamming the door. For two days, she didn't speak to me. She went out alone, came back late in the evening, and acted as if I were invisible. Her mother tried to get me to explain what had happened. I told her I didn't know anything. Then one evening, she came back to show me a poem titled 'He's nice, admit, but hypocrite.' I got the message, but I treated it like any other poem. We became friends again, just like before. One evening, her father came to me and asked if I would be interested in a job at the bank where he worked and oversaw the office.

'But I'm studying. I want to take the bar exam,' I told him.

'You can do that in the evenings or through correspondence,' the man replied.

I weighed the situation carefully, realized he was right, and transferred my courses to correspondence. With a good job at the Commerce Bank and more optimism than before, I started courting Jeni. By fall, we got married."

"Then why did you separate?" comrade Mănoiu wanted to know.

Comrade Bărbulescu paused for a moment as if searching

his memory for a significant moment to continue his story.

"For the best, really. Jeni wanted a child right after we got married, but I opposed it. I wanted children, too, but not while we were living with her parents. They were decent people, I have nothing bad to say about them, and they helped us a lot, but if we didn't respect their opinions, they would get upset, thinking we were ungrateful. Jeni was in her final year of university, and I still had years of work ahead. The times were tumultuous, and I was troubled that in the family, my opinion mattered the least. Jeni and her parents decided everything, often without even asking me. When I told her I wanted us to move out of her parent's home, she opposed it. But I was determined. 'I'm moving out,' I told her. 'If you don't come with me, it won't be my choice.'

'Go! Go to hell if you want! I'm staying here!' she replied.

I left that same day. Her father was my boss at work. I told him we were separating and handed in my resignation. He tried to keep me, but I packed my things and left. That's how I ended up here, through a friend who worked in the administration."

"And Jeni didn't follow you? Didn't she try to reconcile?" asked comrade Mănoiu.

"She had a hard time finding me. Only when she received the divorce papers did she track me down, and then she begged me to reconcile, agreed to move with me, and asked me to forgive her, but I told her it was too late. Once a shirt is torn, you can't wear it as if it were new. In the end, she understood."

"Do you know what happened to her? Did she remarry?"

"Yes, she's fine now. She's teaching at the university."

On the following day, November 7th, the Great October Socialist Revolution in Russia was celebrated, and all the major buildings in the Capital were adorned with portraits of the leaders of the Romanian Workers' Party, led by comrade Gheorghe Gheorghiu-Dej, along with banners proclaiming, "Long Live November 7th." Similar preparations were made at the factory, with new portraits, garlands, and slogans added to the ones already on display on the administrative building's facade and within each department. All employees were informed that the next morning, each employee should arrive at the factory prepared for the grand popular demonstration in Victory Square.

After parting from his colleagues, Dan was on his way to the gate when Crina, his supervisor, caught up with him. Speaking as she walked, without looking at him, she said,

"After the parade tomorrow, come by my house for lunch; my husband is coming back next week." Without waiting for a reply, she moved on toward the tram station.

**Wednesday, November 7**

When Dan arrived at the factory in the morning, the employees were gathered outside on the street, and numerous placards with slogans, flags, and photographs fastened to long wooden poles leaned against the fence, awaiting the designated bearers who would carry them in front of the official stands. Party and union organizers urged everyone to take one of the items as they hurriedly formed the parade columns that would walk the entire distance to Victory Square. Dan searched the crowd for a familiar face, especially those in his group, who were aligned toward the front of the column. Along the way, he spotted the blonde girl from the tooling section and, a little further ahead, Crina and comrade Bărbulescu. He joined them. It was a splendid late autumn morning, promising sunshine and a clear sky. Sorin Petrescu, accompanied by comrade Mănoiu, also joined the group. At last, after all the propaganda materials had been distributed, the group began moving. At every major intersection, new columns of demonstrators merged from the left and right, forming a stream of people flowing in the same direction and pace as the Dâmbovița River.

As they reached Cotroceni Bridge, the column was halted, waiting for the local groups to go ahead. Along the way, tables were set outside in front of restaurants, offering boiled wieners, which had been absent from stores for some time, fresh white bread baguettes, mustard, and bottles of lemonade. Along the sidewalks, lines of people stood at intervals, ensuring no one left the columns. The sun rose high, reflecting off the foreheads of demonstrators glistening with sweat. From time to time, ambulances stationed by the roadside stood ready for the inevitable fainting spells of comrades unaccustomed to such long walks in the heat.

At Izvor Bridge, comrade Nestorescu joined in, having waited there, knowing the route would be passing by. He shook hands with each person and inserted himself between Dan and comrade Bărbulescu.

"I heard on Radio Free Europe that the Soviets have sent tanks into Budapest. There are over 2,500 dead. Across Europe, there are demonstrations against Russia. Many are accusing the Americans of not sending troops there," he said, looking directly at them.

Sorin nudged him with his elbow.

"What did he say?"

"What you were saying the other day: that things aren't good in Hungary. There are worldwide protests against Russia."

"And we are kissing here their butts!"

When they reached Union Square, floods of people poured in from all directions, and groups of activists sought to direct the priority of certain columns over others that needed to continue on

Magheru Boulevard. Heat, noise, exhaustion. The hours of waiting, the activist cordons that prevented anyone from leaving the columns, even for personal necessity, had become unbearable. And there was still a long way to go to reach the tribunes. Only around midday did the factory group finally parade enthusiastically before the officials in the stands, each one trying to glimpse, in their hasty steps, the faces in the central tribune, especially that of comrade Gheorghiu-Dej.

Not far from the tribunes, just beyond the Aviators' statue, was the entrance to Stalin Park, but police cordons blocked entry as the evacuation of thousands of people was organized in a single direction along Floreasca Street. No trams or buses were running at that hour, so the journey home had to be made on foot. As they walked through the neighborhood of houses and small streets, the orderly columns dispersed, with people branching off and some opting to stop at an open restaurant or café for the luxury of a seat, a glass of water, and a moment's rest.

Dan continued walking when someone pulled at his sleeve.

"Let me hold onto you; I'm so tired," said comrade Mănoiu.

"Of course, no problem," Dan said obligingly, offering her his arm.

"There's no shade on this entire street to cool off. What an ordeal, what an ordeal. No one even told us to wear more comfortable shoes. How could they do this?"

"Quite easily. The comrades arrived by limousines at the tribune, will leave exhausted from sitting on their chairs doing nothing. They are envying us for having the freedom to walk," Dan replied.

"Really? I don't live far from here. I'll show you were. Come and rest a bit. My husband might not be home, but that doesn't matter. We're not living in a forest," she said.

"I'm sorry, comrade Mănoiu, but I'm invited to lunch at a friend's place," Dan excused himself.

"A lady friend?" comrade Mănoiu asked with a wink.

"Just a friend."

Her house looked like a villa surrounded by trees, sheltered by a fence that concealed the yard. From there, Dan went alone toward Crina's house, which was hard to reach since demonstrators were still flowing through the main streets. It was past three o'clock when he arrived. He rang at the entrance but received no answer. To pass the time until she arrived, Dan went to the Botanical Garden, which was shady, and sat on a bench. Without realizing it, he fell asleep, leaning against the bench's backrest. When he awoke, his Pobeda watch showed the hour four o'clock. This time, Crina opened the door.

## Sunday, November 11

Everything Dan knew about classical music stemmed from the government's speaker mounted in his aunt's house, which played continuously each day until midnight. Setting foot in the Romanian Athenaeum for the first time, he was filled with inexplicable excitement at the thought that, thanks to Crina, he was entering a world meant for the privileged. A few minutes after he arrived, Crina appeared, dressed in great elegance, and, taking tickets from her purse, handed him one, leading him inside. The opulence of the circular ceiling adorned with painted relief garlands and all the details Dan observed around him made him feel small and insignificant in the grandeur of the hall. He sat beside Crina, who pulled out a note and handed it to him, whispering:

"Please don't be upset with me, Dan, but I ordered you a suit from the Fashion House on Victory Avenue. Stop there Monday to get fitted. Here's the address."

At that moment, the conductor took the stage, and the music drowned out any other sounds in the hall. The opening piece, a premiere, didn't move Dan much, and the next, with its national style, seemed like a medley of familiar folk dances. However, Chopin's Piano Concerto No. 1, which closed the first half of the program, captivated him so deeply that he wished he could listen to it over and over. At intermission, they went out together to the elegant lobby with its winding staircases at the room's ends. Crina excused herself for a few minutes, and he was pleased to take the opportunity to closely examine the lobby's intricate details. As he walked among people, he noticed the blonde woman from the tool-and-die department across the hall, alone, holding a program.

"Good morning," said Dan. "You here?"

"Yes, I love classical music. My mother used to take me here for concerts when I was young. I didn't know you were a fan too."

"Neither did I," Dan laughed. "This is my first concert. Back in the village, I grew up listening to the local folk band. But here, the music is something completely different. I really enjoyed the piano concerto."

"Yes, Chopin is beautiful. I think you'll like Beethoven's symphony coming up just as much."

"I'm glad we ran into each other. May I know your name?" Dan asked.

"Rozica Şfarţ. And yours?"

"Daniel Cristescu. May I call you Rozica?"

"Of course, Dan. I must go; my seat is on the balcony. Goodbye."

"Goodbye, Rozica."

As they parted, Dan began looking for Crina, but she was already behind him.

"Who's that girl?" Crina asked. "Doesn't she work in the factory?"

"Yes, she's a designer in the tool-making department, I think. Her name's Rozica Șfarț."

"Are you two friends?"

"Oh, no. She just told me her name now. It's the first time we've spoken."

"She's young. And very beautiful. After the concert, you're coming over for dinner. I have a little surprise for you, you'll see! And... it may be the last time you can visit; my husband is returning in the next few days. He has many connections; I'll ask him to help find you a small apartment."

A few harmonious chimes signaled the audience to return to their seats. The second half of the concert. Beethoven's Third Symphony, the Eroica, left a lasting impression on Dan as he tried to unravel its story, imagining the tale the composer intended to convey. But the concert program mentioned nothing of the sort. He began to feel as if a bruise had risen on his forehead for all the world to see: his lack of education. His knowledge was limited to what he had learned in school, only the bare minimum required of a person in society. But it wasn't enough. Throughout time, people had created incredible beauty, like this building, like the music he'd heard today, like plays, books, and so many things he hadn't even encountered yet. There was so much to learn! He resolved to begin a systematic study, to read, to visit museums, and to cultivate himself.

Back at Crina's, the surprise was a cardboard box containing a pair of brand-new shoes and three pairs of fine men's socks. She watched joyfully as Dan opened the gifts, encouraging him to try on the shoes to see if they fit. Dan, however, placed the box back on the table, a bit unsettled.

"Please don't be offended, but I'm overwhelmed by these gifts, which I simply can't accept. I can't take these, nor the suit you ordered, unless we agree on one condition: you tell me how much they cost and let me pay you back in installments to the last penny."

"But why, dear Dan? I bought them with all the affection I have."

"I know, and I'm grateful. But it makes me feel diminished in my own eyes. Crina, we're friends, and I want us to remain friends. I fully appreciate your sincerity and the care with which you bought these things, but I can't accept anything I can't repay with equal value. We must remain two equal, independent individuals. Do you understand?"

"As you wish, Dan. Alright… Now, I'll go prepare the meal, and you can pour the wine."

**Monday, November 12**

The following morning, arriving at the factory, Dan found comrade Bărbulescu leafing through the morning paper at his desk. He greeted him with a handshake.

"What's new?" asked Bărbulescu.

"Not much, but I'd like to discuss a personal issue and a work-related one," Dan replied.

"Let's start with the personal one."

"Until now, I hadn't realized how much I lack in terms of general knowledge. I feel like a hollow pastry, inflated but empty inside. I need to read more history, literature, art, and who knows what else. I need a plan but don't know where to begin."

Bărbulescu regarded Dan with interest. After a moment of thought, he said,

"That sounds like a lifelong plan. None of us know everything we should. But from experience, I can offer you some practical advice. Do you know the Russian church with the golden domes behind Mihai Viteazu's statue? The first building on the left of the church on that street is the Russian library. It's rich in books and albums on all disciplines; you can study there. Don't read at random; if, for example, you want to know French literature, go through the writers in chronological order, like you learned Romanian literature. Do the same with painting, architecture, and everything else. That's how I did it. Now, what's the other issue?"

"I believe we could apply a cutting plan for the laminated materials into bars. If we combine longer and shorter pieces based on a well-thought-out plan, we could significantly reduce material consumption."

"Yes, but many of these are cut directly on the machining tools, like screws, nuts, and others."

"Yes, but there are also other materials. For instance, with angles from one bar, we get several of the same part with an end loss that's slightly smaller than the length of the respective part. But if we combine it with a shorter one, the end loss would be much smaller, right?"

"Have you tested this on any specific material types to see what could be achieved with your proposal?"

"Not yet. I wanted to hear your opinion first."

"I think the idea is good. Take a material type, make the cutting plan as you suggest, and compare how many bars are needed in each case. You might be right. Give it a try. Good luck!"

Dan immediately got to work. He had a productive day. By

combining long and short parts from the same material type, the results were significant, depending on the quantity of parts manufactured from the same material. However, for types with limited usage, the results weren't as impactful. Still, even though there was more work ahead, he saw the potential in his proposal.

At the end of the day, he planned to visit the House of Fashion, where Crina had ordered his suit, and being in the city center, he wanted to stop by the library recommended by comrade Bărbulescu for a firsthand look.

Leaving the factory, he joined the throng of people gathered at the tram stop. Often, the tram rides during shift changes at the factory turned into a struggle due to the overcrowding in the cars, where passengers were squeezed like sardines, some even hanging onto bars on the entry steps. Accidents often happen, but few people knew about them, as the press rarely mentioned such issues. Dan couldn't board the first tram due to the crush of people. When the tram left the station, he had a better chance with the next tram, now at the front of the line. But by the time a new tram showed up, another throng had gathered, and again, a crowd piled in, even before the tram arrival. He felt fortunate he could walk home and not have to endure this kind of fight every day.

When the tram finally arrived, those between the doors pushed to get closer, shoving aside others waiting in the line to reach inside. Dan realized that he'd have to fight for a spot and managed to grab hold of a bar in the first-class section. Glancing behind him, he noticed the blond hair of the girl from the drafting board. He reached out his free hand to her; she grasped it, and he helped her up onto the car's step-in front of him. They finally stood together on the platform by the ticket booth, pressed close in the crowded car. Rozica thanked Dan, who continued shielding her by bracing himself against a bar.

"Where are you off to? I've never seen you on the tram before," she asked.

"To a tailor on Victory Avenue, then to a library near the University to look through some books."

"I think I know it. The one by the Russian church?"

"Yes, exactly. It's my first time there. It came recommended."

"I go there often. You'll like it. What are you looking to read?"

"A bit of everything. I have no idea yet. I want to improve my general knowledge, as I feel I'm lacking." Dan admitted. "And you? Where are you headed?"

"Home. I live at Rosetti Square."

"Could I ask if you live alone or with someone?"

"Alone for now. My husband is in prison."

"I'm sorry to hear that."

"Don't worry about it."

The tram continued along the Dâmbovița River. Dan needed to get off near the Operetta Theatre, and she would continue two stops further to Nations Square. They started to work their way toward the front.

"When will I see you again?" asked Dan.

"Perhaps tonight at the library." Dan smiled and instinctively squeezed her shoulders lightly. "Then I'll hold off on 'goodbye' for now—until later." He told her as he got off.

She repeated softly, "Until later."

At the House of Fashion, Master Dobre showed him the fabric Crina had selected. It was indeed splendid. Threads of blue, white, and black formed a discreet, elegant grayish-blue blend. It was fine, lightweight wool that didn't crease. The master took Dan's measurements, showed him the fashionable style Crina had chosen, and told him to return in a few days for a fitting. Satisfied, Dan headed to the library.

The building was large and old, with a wide wrought-iron door leading into a reading room filled with wide tables, each lined with lamps whose green-tinted shade softened the light. Along the walls, shelves stretched up with books protected behind glass-framed doors. At one end of the room sat a librarian woman, discreetly helping and answering visitors' requests.

Entering, Dan stopped at the desk to inquire about a book on the history of art. The librarian directed him to a row of cabinets by the entrance, filled with drawers holding alphabetized index cards. He went to the drawer marked "A" and began searching through cards listing book titles, authors, and chapter details. He wrote down the call number of the book he wanted and handed it to the librarian. While waiting for the book, he glanced around the room; Rozica hadn't arrived yet.

With the book in hand, he settled at the first table by the librarian, switched on the lamp, and began leafing through the pages. It looked like a classical Greek architecture manual, with details on Athens' temples, supported by marble columns of different types, alongside descriptions of the friezes and statues of gods adorning these structures. More than satisfied with his choice, he asked the librarian for a piece of paper and a pencil, then returned to his seat and began studying. That's where Rozica found him, settling at the table across from him. She pulled out the book she'd been reading and sank into it, her back against the chair. Now and then, their gazes met, sparking smiles.

Later that evening, around eight, when the books needed to

be returned, they left the library together, walking through the boulevard lit by streetlamps and the headlights of cars whizzing by. In silence, they reached the corner of the intersection, and when she noticed he intended to walk her home, she remarked:

"If you come, all I can offer is tea and biscuits."

Only then did Dan realize he hadn't eaten much all day. Smiling, he accepted, "Tea and biscuits sound wonderful."

They arrived at a four-story building with an imposing door. They climbed a few steps to the first level, and Rozica unlocked a door leading into a hallway. She unlocked another door, and Dan entered a spacious room with a piano in one corner, plush carpets over a lemon-colored parquet floor, armchairs, a dining table with chairs, and a crystal chandelier with multiple arms hanging from the ceiling. Rozica motioned for him to sit in an armchair and disappeared through the door they'd entered. She reappeared moments later, bringing an electric teapot, some saucers, cups, and a packet of Lica biscuits. Seeing her, Dan felt sheepish.

"I didn't mean to trouble you. I didn't realize it would cause so much work," he said.

She placed the dishes on the table and plugged in the teapot. "It's no trouble. I'm glad to do it. Give us a chance to talk. I don't have many people to chat with."

"Do you play the piano?"

"I used to. I wanted to be a concert pianist. Fate had other plans."

"What happened?"

"Well, we are Jews. Then the war started, and the Germans came. My father, a liberal journalist, refused forced labor. They caught him, arrested him, and he was never seen again. My mother, a singer with a beautiful voice, was forbidden from performing. We survived thanks to family and friends, but three years ago, she got cancer and passed away. She wanted to see me settled, so she married me off. My husband was a fervent Zionist; he organized illegal departures to Palestine, or Israel, as it's called now, and he's wasting away in prison. That's all there is to it. Excuse me, I think the tea is ready."

"And how did you go from being a pianist to a draftswoman?"

"People from the old bourgeoisie like me had to retrain. I had the choice of becoming a lathe operator, a tractor driver, or a drafter. I chose to be a drafter. Would you like to come to the table?"

Dan sat down at the table.

"What sentence did your husband get?"

"Fifteen years, though, who knows if he'll survive until

then."

Dan was shaken by this young woman's story.

"I never imagined you were this strong. What you've told me makes my blood boil. How can the world be so unjust? I'm just a stranger to you, but if you ever think I can help you in any way, please don't hesitate."

"I know, Dan. That's why I chose to talk to you. What you've learned tonight, nobody else knows, and it must stay that way. I think we could be friends."

"Without a doubt. I should go now. When will I see you again?"

"Thursday evening, if you'd like to come with me to a concert at the radio broadcast center?"

"I'd love to, but I don't know where it is..."

"Come pick me up at six. We'll go together."

"I will. Good night!"

"Good night."

**Thursday, November 15th**

Comrade Nestorescu dropped a bombshell: his sweetheart, Pisicuța, agreed to marry him. The arrangements were already made, the paperwork submitted, and the wedding was scheduled for 11 a.m. Thursday morning at Sector 5 City Hall. The whole group was invited, though only Dan, along with Comrades Istrate and Mănoiu, could attend. The others—Sorin and Comrade Bărbulescu—had to stay back to handle any issues that might come up. Dan and the two comrades took the tram from the factory and went together. Along the way, they stopped by a flower shop, each contributing toward a lovely bouquet chosen by the ladies.

The ceremony was beautiful, rather formal, with many attendees, likely guests from other weddings scheduled for that day. A few former colleagues of Comrade Nestorescu in M.A.I. (The Ministry of Internal Affairs) uniforms came as guests. After receiving their marriage certificate and taking photos, everyone was invited to the M.A.I. restaurant for a small celebration. Dan would have preferred not to go, but his two colleagues insisted, so he had no choice.

The restaurant, set in a private house in the center of town, like a former club, was arranged with a table for about 15 people, laden with every possible delicacy. Before long, small shot glasses of țuica loosened tongues and appetites alike. Dan, seated between the two comrades, was bombarded from both sides with jokes, observations, and gossip.

Mrs. Mănoiu, very talkative, used her voice, hands, and even her foot under the table to emphasize her thoughts. At one point, she lamented that there was no music, as she would have loved to dance with Dan. To be more persuasive, she began stroking his leg under the tablecloth. More reserved, Crina kept glancing to see what was happening on Dan's other side without saying a word.

After the main course, Oltenian sausages with fried potatoes, pickles, and Cotnari wine, Dan excused himself, claiming he had an urgent matter to attend to. However, he was met with protests, especially from Comrade Mănoiu, so he stayed a bit longer. Crina managed to whisper to him that her husband, the colonel, had returned from Timişoara and had promised to inquire about a studio apartment for Dan.

When they were leaving, Comrade Mănoiu pleaded with Dan to escort her home as she wasn't feeling well, but he told her that he absolutely couldn't as he had a pressing engagement. It was already past five in the afternoon, and he didn't want to disappoint Rozica, to whom he had promised to attend the radio concert that evening.

Upon arriving, he rang, and Rozica came to open the door. It was still early, and she asked if he would like a coffee.

"Sure, if you'll have one too."

"Of course, I don't plan to fall asleep at the concert."

Dan laughed.

"Don't worry; I'll be right next to you. I'll serve as your best pillow."

"Maybe," Rozica replied, leaving the room.

Dan stood from his seat and began examining the objects around him. The beautifully polished grand piano was covered with a handmade piece, and in the center sat a framed photo of Rozica in a wedding dress, wearing a veil with a crown, resting her head on the shoulder of a young, pleasant-looking man.

When she returned with a tray bearing two steaming coffee cups and a small plate of biscuits, Dan asked:

"Do you still play the piano?"

"Yes, but only during the day. My home has been invaded by impolite people who make my life miserable. They occupy my house, share my bathroom and kitchen, dirty everything, leave dishes in the sink, and then criticize me for waking up too early, coming home too late, or playing the piano when they want to sleep. I think they're trying to force me out. What can I do?"

After finishing her coffee, Rozica went into the other room to change. When she returned, she was dressed in a black dress that covered her ankles, with a discreet amber bead necklace around her neck, matching her blonde hair cascading in waves down her back.

"Do I look all right?"

Dan admired her fair, soft skin and the dress that hugged her slender waist, highlighting her delicate form and graceful movements.

"You always look lovely. But right now, you look stunning."

"I'm glad you approve. I think we should go. The tram stop is just outside; maybe it's less crowded now..."

The tram stop was indeed just outside her house. She was dressed in a black coat, with matching gloves and a purse in her hand. Dan was still wearing his navy pinstripe suit and went hatless. The tram was full but not crowded, and they stood together on the rear platform by the fare collector. Rozica gazed out the window at the places the tram passed, and Dan encircled her waist, enclosing her with his arms on the bar surrounding the platform. At one point, she turned to him and said, "Thank you for being with me." Dan felt a lump in his throat, not knowing why, surprised that he could be so moved.

They entered the crowded hall, helped Rozica leave her coat in the cloakroom, and took their seats. They sat side by side, with him trying to understand the Italian-sounding terms in the program. He wanted to ask Rozica but couldn't do so during the concert, and he was embarrassed to reveal his cultural gaps. He resolved to look up each term at the library the next day, pleased to realize that there was a treasure trove of information at his disposal.

The music seemed to seep into his soul like the air he breathed, helping to clear his thoughts with a sense of calm and clarity.

On the way back, as Rozica searched for the keys in her purse, Dan told her it was late, and he'd be going home. As the tram approached, Rozica kissed him on the cheek and let him go.

**Friday, November 16**

During the lunch break, Dan went to visit Rozica in her office, where comrade Rosner, secretary to chief engineer comrade Budău, was locked in a heated dispute with comrade Răcaru. He had the audacity to say that she'd remained an "old maid" because she couldn't stop talking and always had something to nitpick.

"It's none of your business to call me an old maid, first of all," comrade Rosner shot back irritably, typing away. "Maybe I just didn't want to marry a brute like you. Maybe the man I chose didn't live to see another day; God rest his soul, and I didn't want to marry anyone else. What do you know about me? Hmm?"

She paused, reached into her bag under the desk, and pulled out a handkerchief. Comrade Răcaru stayed silent. He was the designer responsible for the projects Rozica would ink. Dan moved closer to her drafting table, watching the steady line of ink glide under her pen.

"Quite the scene," he commented.

"He's always needling her. I don't know what he's got against her."

"I wanted to thank you for last night's concert. The Pastoral Symphony—such beautiful music. I could listen to it over and over again."

Rozica nodded.

"I haven't asked—when will I see you again?"

"I don't know. What do you suggest?"

"I haven't thought about it yet. I want to check with comrade Nestorescu and see if he has any theater tickets. Would you be interested?" She smiled and nodded. "All right, I'll leave you to it, then. Goodbye!"

"Goodbye!"

In truth, comrade Mănoiu's description of comrade Nestorescu held a grain of truth: he had a knack for squeezing money out of stones. His contributions to the group of material efficiency were almost negligible. He could barely read a technical drawing, much less a complex assembly, and he did his calculations with pencil and paper, often figuring the results off the top of his head. But with his open, mild, and eternally smiling demeanor, he charmed everyone, always surrounded by friends. He had connections with those who provided payroll-deducted tickets for theater, opera, and film premieres and worked as a tour guide with O.N.T. Carpați on organizing mountain group trips, especially for skiers in the winter. He loved the good life, sharing a glass of wine and chatting about everything without offending or getting into controversies. Dan went to see him, hoping for some good tickets. Comrade Nestorescu pulled a few tickets from an envelope, spreading them on the desk. The problem was Dan didn't know what to choose.

"Which one would you recommend?" he asked.

"Depends, drama or comedy?"

"Something interesting. I'm not going alone."

Comrade Nestorescu understood, offering him two tickets to "The Inspector General" featuring Alexandru Giugaru at the National Theater for Sunday evening. As Dan was about to leave, comrade Nestorescu motioned for him to wait.

"Would you be interested in joining a rotating mill?"

"What's that?" Dan asked.

"A sort of mutual fund, like the C.A.R. (The House of Reciprocal Help, a Union funded organization). Ten of us contribute 50 lei every payday and draw lots to decide who gets the whole 500 lei each round. What do you think?"

"Interesting idea. You said we draw lots for the order? I could use 600 lei…"

"It's attainable if we have twelve in the group. Should I put you on the list?"

"Who else do you have?"

"No one yet. You're the first I've asked."

"All right, let's see how it turns out…"

That afternoon, Dan met Rozica at the library, and while walking home that evening, he told her about the tickets he'd secured. It was a dark, windy November evening. Dan was still wearing a light wool coat, hardly suitable for the cold weather, while Rozica had a winter wool coat and a headscarf tied under her chin, keeping her hair from whipping in the wind. Dan wrapped an arm around her shoulders, pulling her close. She matched his step and then said,

"I've been wanting to see that play. It's by a Russian writer, Gogol. It's a good comedy, a satire."

On the way home on the tram, Dan thought how wonderful it would be if his new suit, promised by the fashion house for the following week, would be ready in time for their night at the theater. He decided to call comrade Dobre in the morning to check, aiming for a time when his boss wouldn't be in the office. The foreman checked and then confirmed that Dan could pick it up before the workshop closed on Saturday evening. "Good," thought Dan, "That's one problem solved. Now, what do I do about my winter coat? It doesn't go with the suit…"

**Sunday, November 18**

Dan's aunt couldn't quite understand what was happening to him; he'd changed again, especially after the ordeal he'd been through following that girl's death.

"It's only been a few weeks, yet his cheeks have regained color, and he's got his old energy back. He leaves at the crack of dawn and comes home late, around nine or even ten, eats everything on his plate, and says he has a lot to study. Claims he's at the library every day. I asked him, 'What do you need to read for, dear? You don't have any exams!' And he said he doesn't know enough, which is why he's reading. Who am I to say he's wrong? And now, look, he's turned up in this fine new suit, a gentleman's suit. Where's he getting these fancy tastes from? His father's a simple man and still wears his old peasant shoes because they're comfortable. But he just stays quiet and doesn't say a thing. Maybe that's how it should be."

Dan was almost ready to go pick up Rozica, dressed in his new suit, which fit like a glove, with a pressed white shirt, a tie, and brand-new polished shoes. Clothing had never made him feel either superior or inferior, but now this new suit felt as though it opened new possibilities, like the magic hat that lets you go unnoticed among the emperor's courtiers. He put on his heavy wool peasant jacket and headed to the tram.

Rozica opened the door, dressed in a housecoat over butter-colored silk pajamas. Once inside the living room, Dan removed his jacket, and Rozica couldn't hide her surprise.

"You look completely different tonight! Let me take a good look at you."

She circled him admiringly, then took his hand and led him to her bedroom, where a grand wardrobe with a full-length crystal mirror stood. She took a gray wool overcoat off a hanger and helped him put it on. It fits him perfectly. Then she handed him a pair of leather gloves and a silk scarf.

"Now you look like a prince. If I weren't married, I'd marry you myself."

Dan admired himself in the wardrobe mirror, then removed the overcoat to return it to her.

"No, keep it. It's yours," she said.

"I can't; it belongs to your husband. I have my jacket. Once I've paid off my debts, I'll buy a coat like this."

"No, Dan. Who knows when my husband will return? In the meantime, the moths will get to it. It's yours."

"No! Don't insist. You're making me regret coming."

"At least for tonight. Will you indulge me?"

"All right. Just for tonight."

"Come to the other room for a coffee."

They returned to the living room. She prepared the coffee in the kitchen and came back with a tray of cups and saucers, sitting beside him on the sofa.

"You know, Dan, it's been a long time since I left the convent."

Dan looked at her, puzzled, unsure what she meant. She continued,

"I mean, I'm no saint. You could even call me a whore, like any other woman who gives herself to a man for material comfort. I've had three: one to continue my piano career; he didn't keep his promise. Another is for a better grade to get my draftsman's certificate. And another to keep these two rooms, which used to be mine. That's who you're dealing with. I wanted you to know so you'd stop treating me like a saint."

"You're not telling me anything I didn't already know, dear. If we're laying our cards on the table, I'm no better. I prostitute myself just like you. See this suit? It was bought by a lady who could be my mother. She caught me in a tight spot and took advantage. I promised to pay it off to the last penny, but I haven't given her a single coin yet. My conscience stings like a swarm of bees. I'm no better than you."

"I'd hoped to stay chaste, but I had to make concessions. Maybe the time has come to pay for my sins…" she said.

"What do you mean?"

"That my husband is rotting in a prison in Târgu-Mureş, and it's uncertain if he'll get out alive. He still has another ten years or so, and by then, I might not feel anything for him. I think I've fallen in love with you."

"I feel the same. I didn't think it was possible again, but it's happened."

"Really? Do you love me?"

"I think so. More than I thought I could. It's complicated; not long ago, I loved a girl who chose to end her life rather than unite it with mine. She was violated by a scoundrel and couldn't bear living, knowing she'd been defiled by another. She poisoned herself because of it."

"And with that girl, were you as distant as you are with me?"

"Are you asking if I had a sexual relationship with her? No. I knew we'd marry soon. I didn't want to rush things; I wanted to take her as she was, pure. I respect you, too, as a married woman, and I don't want you to blame me for ruining your life. That doesn't mean I don't desire you. You have no idea how much space you take up in my thoughts. If it wasn't too late right now, I'd prove to you that you're wrong."

"Will you stay after the show tonight?"

"I'm afraid not. I must go home. My aunt won't sleep all night if I don't come back. I don't want to upset her; she's already got enough on her plate."

"Then forget the tickets. Prove to me now, darling, that I'm wrong!"

**Monday, November 19th**

"Damn hooligans! I'll show you!" were the words of Chief Engineer Budău after a prank by one of the norm technicians, who shrunk back behind a desk, not knowing who his victim would be. The entire room erupted in laughter, stifled by hands over mouth so it wouldn't be seen. The technician, a young man with a wealth of tricks up his sleeve and the author of numerous pranks got the idea to tie a 20-lei note to a long piece of string and place it just inside the office door, where he hid behind the furniture and tugged the string. As it happened, the chief engineer himself walked in to discuss something with one of the technologists. When he saw the bill on the floor, he instinctively bent down to pick it up, but the timekeeper pulled the invisible string, and the money slipped from his grasp. He bent down again to grab it, only for it to evade him once more—several times until he realized something wasn't right. We were all in hysterics. But the engineer, a former worker and probably no stranger to such pranks, dismissed it and let the incident slide.

Last night, when Dan returned home, his aunt was waiting with a set table and food kept warm in the oven. Dan changed clothes and sat down to eat.

"Aunt, you wouldn't be upset if sometimes I didn't come home at night, would you?"

"How could I not be upset? What kind of question is that?" the aunt replied.

"Well, how should I put it? There's this girl, a friend I talk to, and sometimes it gets late, so I could stay over there to sleep. You understand?"

"I understand, dear; of course I do. But what kind of girl would let you stay over? She's not one of those, is she…a loose woman?"

"No, Aunt, how could you think that? She's a good girl. If you'd like, I could bring her here sometime so we can meet. She was married…"

"And where's her husband? Dead?"

"No, in prison."

"In prison, dear? What did he do?"

"Politics."

"Lord, protect us! They say these types are even more dangerous than the others, the criminals."

"Not him. He helped people escape from here."

"Escape? Where can you escape from your fate? But tell me, is she one of ours, a Christian?" Dan lowered his head, thinking he'd already said too much. Then, resolutely, he told his aunt,

"Aunt, it doesn't matter what she is. We're friends, I like her, and I want to be with her. That's all." The woman stood up, determined to confront him:

"It's not just that. What do you expect me to tell your father? That I let you go to some heathen? Is this what we struggled for? For you to live in sin with a woman whose man is in prison. I'll send a word for your father tomorrow to come talk sense into you because I'm washing my hands of it. It's not my business anymore, you hear?"

Dan never expected this outcome. It wasn't in his aunt's nature to react this way. To avoid making things worse, he decided to go to bed. When his aunt saw him heading to his bedroom, she said,

"What are you sleeping here for? Don't you have a lover? Go over there!"

"Tomorrow! There are no trams left at this hour."

At lunchtime, he went to see Rozica. It had started to snow outside, and it was cold. They went together into the hall where prototypes of new products were being built. In a corner of the hall, there were tables and benches for the employees' breaks. They sat on the edge of one of them. Her eyes sent messages only he could understand.

"You seem a bit down today," observed Rozica.

"My aunt got upset last night when I told her I might be staying out some nights. She threatened to call my father to come and set me straight."

"And what do you plan to do?"

"I don't know. You see, it's not so much that you're married or that your husband is where he is. It's the fact that you're not Christian. They could manage with the other things but with this… What will people say when they find out?"

"I know. It's the same for us."

"I think my father would be more understanding, but my aunt… I've been living with her for years; she practically raised me. I didn't want to upset her, and now she can't even look at me. I don't know what to do."

"Do you want to move somewhere else?"

"Where? I want to pay off my debt for clothes first. It's a complicated situation."

"We'll see. Let's talk tonight at the library, alright?"

"Alright."

They parted ways. Back in the office, he asked Comrade Nestorescu if he knew anyone with a room for rent. Nestorescu first wanted to know what had happened since things had seemed fine until now. Dan said he'd had an argument with his aunt and couldn't stay there anymore. His comrade promised to investigate. Dan went back to work but without much enthusiasm. Crina nudged his shoulder from behind with a ruler, and Dan turned to face her.

"Take this report, read it, and check if it's correct, then bring it to the typist." Dan took the report, holding a few pages together with a paperclip. The second page was meant for him: "I haven't seen you in a while. The studio my husband promised seems delayed. Don't you know where we could meet? I miss you; I think I'll arrange a provincial trip for the two of us. What do you say? Bye."

Dan let the report fall to the floor, and bending down, he slipped the note meant for him into his pocket and took the report to the typist. Passing by Rozica, he gave her a furtive smile.

**Tuesday, November 20th**

After the discussion with his aunt, this was about the second night in a row Dan found sleep escaping him, sticking to his eyelids only briefly before vanishing again: first due to anger, and now due to his closeness with Rozica. Knowing her to be so close in this bed with its soft mattresses and silky sheets was a revelation for Dan, who had grown used to rough hemp sheets and a hard bed of packed wool. Each touch of her body stirred unusual sensations within him, igniting new desires that Rozica accepted willingly.

In the morning, when he needed to go to the bathroom with a new toothbrush Rozica had given him and wearing her husband David's bathrobe, the bathroom door was locked. He waited in the shared hallway, and when it was finally free, a woman slightly past middle age emerged wearing only a loose slip that barely concealed her chest and rounded figure. She stopped, surprised, to look at Dan, trying to guess whether he was the husband or someone else.

On their way to the factory, they got off the tram at Lazăr Lyceum and walked toward Izvor Bridge to continue along the Dâmbovița River. Sitting side by side in the tram, they were noticed by some colleagues from the factory who greeted them or exchanged a few words. With his thick woolen coat, hat, gloves, and hand-knitted scarf, Dan looked more like a townsman from the free market than anything else. Only his manners, especially around Rozica, seemed to set him apart.

At the factory, they each went to their respective offices and resumed their daily activities. Sorin couldn't hold back long before asking,

"Who was that girl you were talking to on the tram?"

"A colleague from the Tooling Department."

"She's pretty. Introduce me to her sometime?"

"You're a bit late. She's taken. I mean, married."

"Hmm. A girl like that, though… That's just my type. What do you think? No jokes, now, how do you think a woman would look at someone like me?"

"Sorin, you're better than millions of men out there. Any woman would be proud to have you. Trust me, you're not one to pass up!"

"Well, in that case, find me one!"

"You want me to find you a girl? Have your mother find you one!"

They both laughed. Dan turned toward Comrade Istrate:

"Have you heard anything about Comrade Ştefan's proposal? I'd like to give him some good news."

"No, Dan. I'm not sure what Comrade Voinea, the director, has done about it. I'll have to ask. Anyway..."

"Yes, and the plans for bar-cutting have been put into practice yet..."

"That'll happen when a new order goes into production. Patience: you know haste makes waste."

During the lunch break, Comrade Mănoiu came out of the office after Dan and called him over.

"I heard from Comrade Nestorescu that you're looking for a place to rent. I think I can help. In my yard, there's a small house that was used by the servant of the former landlord. I'm using it as storage now, but if you want, I can let you stay there instead. What do you say?"

"But what will your husband think?"

"Oh, he always thinks what I think. That's not an issue."

"Thank you. You know, I'm a bit busy these days. Maybe next week, if it's not too much trouble..."

"No trouble at all, Dan, any time!"

**Saturday, November 24th**

The rotating mill loan set up by Comrade Nestorescu started at the last payday, and since Dan drew the second slot, he's due to receive 600 lei today. It couldn't have come at a better time, as now he could pay off his debt to Crina with enough left over to contribute to household expenses at Rozica's place. It was truly a joy to always be together, and whatever they did, they did with happiness and a feeling of fulfillment, a boundless sense of peace that only rarely graces a person in their lifetime. Between work, the library, and home, they found enough time to go to a movie, listen to music on a phonograph, or enjoy a piano performance just for him, punctuated by tender kisses even mid-performance.

At lunch, Dan went to Comrade Rosner to ask for an envelope and a sheet of paper for a letter. The typist handed them over and watched as that girl, Rozica, left the office with Dan, who now made it a habit to visit her and chat regularly. The typist's heart couldn't bear it, and after the break, when the girl returned, she started questioning her in a shrill voice loud enough for everyone to hear:

"That Comrade Cristescu who keeps coming here. Did you know him before, or did you meet him here?"

"Here."

"Are you friends?"

"Colleagues."

"Then why does he keep coming to see you?"

"I don't know. I haven't asked him."

"Does he know you're of different religions?"

"I don't know."

"Well, be careful, girl, because you know how people are. Once you're the talk of the town, there's no escaping it…"

Dan sat at his desk and wanted to write a few lines to Crina, explaining that the money in the envelope was to cover her expenses on his behalf. He would never forget what she had meant to him, and he would remain forever indebted and grateful. He also wanted to add that he'd bonded deeply with an especially loving and understanding person with whom he was now living and that for this reason, to avoid disappointing her, he couldn't continue the friendship with Crina, which had helped him through an extraordinarily tough period. He wanted to weave all this onto the blank sheet of paper but held back, thinking he might not be able to give it to her that day and to be safe, he tucked the envelope and paper into his pocket.

This time, at the end of the day, he had to wait until Comrade Nestorescu finished collecting the rotating mill loan money for him, and then they left the factory together.

On payday in the street in front of the main gate, the same scene repeated itself with clockwork regularity: many women, some with children in arms or by the hand, positioned themselves near the iron gate, trying not to lose sight of the men who were easily drawn by colleagues for a quick drink, only to arrive home drunk, looking for a quarrel and without a penny left. Ashamed in front of their colleagues, these men would step aside with their wives and negotiate how much to give them and how much to keep for cigarettes and a drink with their comrades.

When Dan exited through the factory gate, an elderly woman dressed in black with her head covered in a scarf came in front of him.

"Auntie, what are you doing here? How long have you been waiting at the gate?" Dan asked.

"What else can I do, Danut, when you never come home anymore? You've completely distanced yourself from us..."

"No, Auntie, I swear it's not like that. But time's short, and the days are even shorter now, and I still have to stand in line for food since no one else can get it for me these days, so that's why..."

"Then why don't you return to where you were, where everything was good, and you had no troubles?"

"I'm staying with this girl now. We're helping each other out. It's better this way."

"But what about all your things? You left everything at my

place. Do you not need them anymore?"

"I'll come by Auntie. If you like, I can come tomorrow since it's Sunday and pick them up."

"Come, dear, come so we can talk, and your father wants to know what's happening with you too."

"I'll come, Auntie, but I'll bring the girl with me…"

"All right, if you think it's for the best."

Dan leaned down to kiss the old woman before parting. Comrade Nestorescu had stood for a moment behind Dan while the woman greeted him, then headed off to catch the tram as it approached the station. Dan watched his aunt cross the Dâmbovița River over the bridge in front of the factory before continuing toward the tram station. In front of the iron gates, there were still many women waiting with their children.

**Monday, November 26**

When Dan entered the office Monday morning, Sorin looked at him with a mischievous smile on his lips.

"You owe us a celebration," he said.

"A celebration? Why?"

"They've given you a nickname. They've baptized you."

"Seriously? What is it?"

"Country Bumpkin. That's what they called you."

"They can go kiss me… And how do you know this?"

"I overheard them. They were even talking about taking up a collection to buy you a yoke to complete your look."

"Who said that?"

"That I'm not telling."

From her desk, comrade Mănoiu waited for a response from Dan, one he delayed giving. He kept his head buried in the papers piled on his desk, glancing her way now and then without wanting to confront her directly. Meanwhile, Dan was waiting for Crina to move from behind him so he could hand her the envelope and letter he'd prepared at home, now tucked away in his coat pocket. When he noticed her rise from her chair, he followed her outside the office.

Sensing him, Crina turned toward him:

"Oh, good to see you, Dan. I might have some good news for you. My husband seems to have arranged a studio apartment with those in charge of housing. This is only temporary because they'll soon start building a new block of apartments behind the Royal Palace. I'll give you the address to go there."

"Crina, thanks, but I don't need it anymore."

"What do you mean you don't need it? After all, did I do for you? Did you find something else?"

"Yes. Here, take this envelope. It explains everything."

Crina took the envelope, opened it, and saw the money inside.

"What's this?"

"My debt to you!"

"Did I ever ask you to pay me back? I don't need it. It was a gift!"

"That I can't accept. I told you before, and you agreed."

"No, I didn't agree. I just didn't want to argue. Take it back!"

Dan pushed away her hand as she tried to return the envelope.

"No! I explained this to you. Your gesture was kind, and I admired it. But I don't accept gifts or wages just because we're friends. That degrades me!"

"Look, people are watching us. And what about the housing?"

"I've moved in with someone."

"A woman? That Jewess from S.D.V.?"

Dan felt a wave of anger, but he decided it was best to take it as a joke.

"If you think I'm the kind of guy who'd live with comrade Rosner, then no!"

"Oh, don't play dumb. You know who I'm talking about. Do you think I haven't noticed? Everyone's talking."

"It doesn't matter! Jewess or not, she's, my friend. I thought you were my friend too. You promised you'd never be a burden, but you forgot!"

He left her standing there, angry and clutching the envelope, and went back to the office.

The day before, around two in the afternoon, Dan had gone with Rozica to his aunt's house in the Grant neighborhood. Dan wanted to show his aunt that Rozica was just like any other girl, no different from the young women she knew and that neither her religion nor the fact she had a husband in prison made her any better or worse than others in similar circumstances.

Now, however, on the way to the old woman's house, he wondered whether it had been a good idea to persuade Rozica to join him here, especially after his aunt's reaction during their last conversation a week prior. But it was too late now. They planned to stay for a few hours before heading to the Giuleşti Theater near Grant Bridge to see a play.

Before entering the house, they carefully brushed the snow

and mud from their shoes on the frozen mat by the entrance. Sensing their arrival, the aunt opened the door, and they entered. Dan kissed her on both cheeks and introduced Rozica. The aunt looked her over thoroughly as the girl removed her coat, revealing a light blue jersey dress that hugged her waist. As Dan hung her coat on the rack, he overheard his aunt ask:

"My dear, why is this girl so thin? Isn't she consumptive?"

Rozica smiled while Dan hurried to assure her otherwise:

"Auntie, she's as healthy as you or me. That's just how she's built."

"She should eat better, really. A woman who isn't strong can't handle things these days. Tell me, girl, do you eat pork?"

The girl smiled again, but Dan jumped in quickly to correct his aunt's words:

"No, Auntie, in her family, pork is forbidden."

But Rozica protested:

"No, Dan. I ate it. I eat everything. I'm not religious."

"Well done, dear. That's how it should be! You're beautiful, and it would be a shame for you to waste without good food. Look, I made some meatball soup and cabbage rolls with sour cabbage and polenta. Dănuţ, dear, will you help me set the table?"

Dan investigated Rozica's eyes, seeing her smiling tolerantly, and went to set the table. After they ate, Dan went to his room to pack the things he needed and changed into the new suit he'd left there. Meanwhile, the aunt stayed with Rozica, asking her questions about her family, her marriage, and her husband's fate.

"But you're so young. How old were you when you got married?"

"I'd just finished high school. I was around 18, maybe almost 19. But my mother insisted. I think she suspected she didn't have much time left."

"And your husband, was he older?"

"He'd just finished university. He was an idealist. After the war, he said all Jews needed to go to Palestine, that their place was there, and to rebuild their country."

"What do you say, dear! And they put him in prison for that?"

"For that, and for collecting funds to help them get there…"

"But he didn't hurt anyone, didn't stab anyone?"

"No! He would never do that. He was just like my father; he fought for justice. I don't think he ever told a lie his whole life."

The aunt remained thoughtful, then rose and began tidying up around her. Rozica asked if she could help, but the old woman objected:

"No, today you're a guest. We'll see another time."

Dan came back, ready to go, as it was time to head to the theater.

"Auntie, we're off now, but after the show, we'll come back for me to change and grab the package from my bed."

"Alright, dear. Alright."

## Saturday, December 1st

For several days, Crina had stopped acknowledging Dan's greetings, and she no longer sent him to the typist with letters, now relying instead on Comrade Nestorescu. Comrade Mănoiu had also shown a change of attitude recently, and Dan began to feel somewhat isolated without knowing why. After hours, Nestorescu suggested meeting at the restaurant near the factory because he had something important to share. The invitation was extended to Comrade Bărbulescu and Sorin as well.

During the break, Dan went to look for Rozica, but she wasn't there. Comrade Rosner told him Rozica had been summoned by the Personnel Office to give a statement.

"Did something happen here? Is she involved?" asked Dan.

"No, dear. It's about her past; you know how things were back then with the wealthy ones."

Dan shrugged, not wanting to continue the conversation.

When his shift ended, he scanned the crowd for Rozica, but not seeing her, he hurried to catch up with Sorin, who walked hunched, with his coat collar turned up to protect his ears from the cold.

"What does Nestorescu want from us?"

"No idea. He just said he had something important to tell me." Replied Dan.

"And I've got something to tell you, too! The two ladies in our group were talking about you the day before yesterday. Mănoiu, the younger one, was fuming. She said she wanted to offer you housing and that you didn't even give her an answer. They blamed it on your girlfriend, saying you're under her spell."

Dan remained silent.

Nestorescu was the first to arrive at the restaurant and ordered a dozen mititei (Romanian style sausages), wine, and soda. Comrade Bărbulescu joined shortly after. Inside, only a couple of tables were occupied. Nestorescu poured wine into their glasses, and Comrade Bărbulescu placed a pack of cigarettes on the table, lighting one up. They raised their glasses with the usual "Cheers."

Nestorescu looked Dan straight in the eyes.

"What high-ranking officials in security do you know?"

"None."

"Do you have any enemies? Did you fall out with anyone who might envy you?"

"Not that I know of."

"You're under investigation. Someone is trying to bury you, claiming you tried to kill a girl after raping her last summer. They say that's why you came to work here, to escape your past."

Dan felt a cold sweat breaking over him. His three colleagues stared at him, waiting for him to say something, as such accusations didn't fit the man sitting with them. Meanwhile, the waiter arrived with bread, mustard, silverware, and a plate of sizzling mititei. Each of them grabbed one with their fork, but Dan chose to drink instead.

"When the story of my office colleague and her alleged assault happened, I wasn't even there. I was in Ploiesti fetching emulsion for the lathes. This is documented and known by everyone. I don't know why they're digging up the past now."

Scenes from that time flashed in Dan's mind, piling one on top of the other like slices of bread.

"That girl was my fiancée, Anişoara. God rest her soul! I

loved no one as much as I loved her. After the assault, Anişoara took her own life. I couldn't stay there anymore, so I came here."

Sorin nudged Dan with his elbow. "Eat before it gets cold."

Dan took a mititel. They ate in silence, deep in thought, without sympathy or regret. After each paid his part, they walked together to the tram station, following their usual route home.

Although Dan initially intended to go straight to Rozica's home, he decided to head to the library, where it was quiet, and he could think. Seated at an empty table, he rested his head in his hands, appearing to read something reflected on the lacquered surface. From Sorin and Nestorescu's accounts, he realized the two women in his group had banded together to conspire against him. Since he had rebuffed their advances, they decided to take revenge, aided by the influential power of their husbands, whom they betrayed shamelessly. No one knew this better than Dan, yet it didn't help at all. People's fates hung so heavily on others' power that truth, justice, and fairness lost all value, becoming mere tools of oppression against the innocent. Those who should have been judges became victims of lawless people who wielded unchecked power.

The notion of justice in the world around him now crumbled like a castle made of sand, leaving behind only a cloud of dense dust that even the sun could not pierce. He felt cornered, like prey surrounded by wolves. If Security reopened the case, trying to pin the blame on him, as Nestorescu hadn't fabricated the rumors he shared, what chance did he have to prove his innocence? Whom could he call as a witness to his innocence? And even if someone came forward, who would have the courage to stand against the army of security forces ordered to punish him? Now that this infernal machine had been set in motion, not even Crina, with all her malign influence, could not stop it if she wanted to. So, he was lost.

With no solution in sight, he got up from the table, realizing he needed to tell Rozica he'd have to return to his aunt. At least she had to be shielded from the attention now focused on him.

Rozica welcomed him warmly, though her face was tense with worry and a restrained need to share the bad news that had suddenly arisen with heavy consequences for both. But not wanting to spoil his mood immediately, she headed to the kitchen to prepare dinner. She soon returned with plates, cutlery, bread, and an omelet sizzling in the pan. On her next trip, she brought the electric kettle and cups for tea. Dan broke the silence.

"I looked for you today. They told me you were called to Personnel for a statement. What statement?"

"I wanted to tell you about it after we ate. I think the neighbors must have reported me for associating with 'suspicious individuals'; they probably meant you and for having excess space as a single person. They might try to throw me out on the street.

They asked me to list all the people I know and explain how I've managed to luxuriate in a space of over 30 square meters, even though I'm entitled to only eight. Tell me, what was I supposed to write?"

Dan was speechless. For the second time, those who hate him find revenge by targeting the innocent people close to him. He saw how his presence in the lives of those close to him was harmful, and he couldn't forgive himself for it. Again, the drama of last summer with Anișoara was repeating itself; just as he couldn't prevent the outcome then, he couldn't see what he could do differently this time. The thought of throwing himself from a window crossed his mind, though he knew he could never actually go through with it. In any case, it was too late to return to his aunt's house, so he began recounting Anișoara's story to Rozica, along with what he had learned from Nestorescu.

By the time he finished, it was nearly morning, but since it was Sunday, they could stay in bed a while longer. Rozica said only this:

"I've heard that life in Israel is different. It's hard there, too, but not like it is here. David was right. I'm starting to feel that's what I should do. Would you come with me?"

"How?"

"We'll find help."

**Sunday, December 2nd**

Dan hadn't slept at all. Lying next to Rozica with his head on the pillow, he stared into the darkness, watching the pale light from the street cast shadows on the ceiling. He pondered her words from before: Israel, the cradle of humanity, the land of the patriarchs, the Holy Land of the people with whom God had forged an eternal covenant, sanctified by the birth of His only Son, Christ the Savior. Would salvation be waiting for him there, too?

Who else but God and the Savior could rescue him from the clutches of those plotting to destroy him and his loved ones physically, morally, and spiritually? Could it be that through Rozica's words, the Lord was sending him a message of salvation at this moment of crisis? How could he refuse the outstretched hand, the path laid out before him? No, this girl's message, her appearance in his life, and the love that bound them, it couldn't be mere chance; it was the hand of Providence, directed by the One who governs all fates. And he had a duty to follow it!

When and how, he wondered? As of now, it seems he isn't under surveillance yet. Tomorrow, at the factory, they might summon him to Personnel to give a statement. Then would come exhausting days of investigation, interrogations, questioning by the union and U.T.M., and possibly even expulsion from those organizations. Then, the risk of arrest or being dismissed as an antisocial element will follow. In conclusion, he had to disappear before Security caught wind, which meant immediately! How and in what way? Rozica mentioned they would find help.

As dawn's light began to fill the bedroom, Dan could no longer lie still. He gently tried to slip out of bed, but Rozica stirred.

"What are you doing, dear? Where are you going?"

"I can't sleep, and I didn't want to wake you."

"I wasn't sleeping either. I don't think I slept at all."

"Neither did I. You know what I was thinking? If we want to go where you said, we must leave now, today!"

"That's what I was thinking too. We should go together but separately. We shouldn't be seen side by side. Pack a few essentials, some papers, and money if you have any, and go as you are, with your short coat and cap. I have an army rucksack I use for hiking, and I'll take what I need and some jewelry from my mother. We can't carry heavy bags."

"You're right. I need to quickly stop by my aunt to let her know I'll be away for a few days. I'll tell her I'm on assignment in Moldova; I don't want her to worry. Then I'll write her a letter to explain."

"Alright, then let's meet at the Gara de Nord (North Railway Station). Pick up a copy of Mersul Trenurilor (Railway schedule) from there; we'll need it. I think we'll have to go to Satu-Mare, and I'm not sure if it might be better to change trains once or twice along the way. I used to know someone there. What do you think?"

"I'm getting dressed now and heading out. How much time do you need before we meet?"

"About two, maybe three hours."

"So, before noon, on the platform near the information office."

Rozica slipped out of bed and wrapped herself in her silk robe. They embraced, eyes brimming with tears, and Dan bolted out the door.

From now on, their only hope lay in God's Will.

# The Return of the Prodigal Sons

David Kimel

# The Parting

Sunday, December 2, 1956. It was still dark outside when Dan burst into the street, leaving Rozica behind, hurrying to catch a tram to his aunt's house. After a sleepless night, consumed by the troubling revelations from Sorin and Nestorescu the day before and, most of all, by Rozica's interrogation at the personnel office, he felt as if the ground beneath him was slipping away, pushing him toward the edge of an abyss with nothing to cling to.

The freezing December morning wind was refreshing as he waited at the tram stop. At such an early hour on a Sunday, the trams wouldn't be as crowded as it was on other days, yet with none in sight coming from Foişorul de Foc (Firefighter's tower), he decided it would be quicker to walk to Lazăr Lyceum, only a couple of stops away. Walking down towards the University, he tried to commit to memory, point by point, everything he'd discussed with Rozica that morning. He had the feeling that no other moment in his life could be as important as what was to happen that day and in the days that would follow, depending on whether their plan would succeed or fail. The obscurity of this plan frightened him, unaccustomed as he was to such risks, yet, lacking other options and as if suspended by a spider's thread, he surrendered to fate with his eyes wide with dread, hoping that God would help him and Rozica overcome the dangers that seemed to be closing in.

As he crossed Calea Victoriei, the streetlamps dimmed, and the darkness began to lift into the gray of a dreary day. Hurring on the boulevard, Dan noticed a few silhouettes slipping along the buildings with their lights off and giant posters advertising the movies at cinemas. Reaching Schitu Măgureanu Street, Dan headed toward Izvor Bridge, to the tram 14 stop, which passed in front of the factory and would take him close to his aunt's home. Once he arrived, Dan cast one last glance at the factory buildings opposite, where he had worked for just a few weeks, though it felt as though years had passed. How was it possible, he wondered, that in such a short time, with no known fault of his own, his fate would turn so suddenly against him, threatening his freedom? He had grown fond of the work he was doing there, of the team he worked with, especially comrade Bărbulescu, Sorin, and even comrade Nestorescu, before whom he now felt guilty, knowing he owed those swept up in Nestorescu's schemes more money than he could ever repay under the current circumstances. Since finishing school that spring, or rather, since starting as a norm technician at the Herăstrău plant, his first employer, events had swept him along like a hurricane, throwing him in different directions with no chance to oppose. Meeting Anişoara there had made Dan feel as if life had taken on a new color, as though he saw everything through colored lenses. The world had suddenly brightened. But when a monster in human skin destroyed Anișoara, the girl with an angelic face and contagious joy, Dan felt the eclipse of his own world, not just his hope, but all his dreams too. He was so devastated that he could no longer work there. Then, at the Metallurgical Plant on the banks of the Dâmbovița River, he happened to meet Rozica. A descendant of an affluent Jewish intellectual family, orphaned of her father after the war and her mother after the Communists took power, she saw her husband imprisoned for political reasons, envied and treated with antisemitic hostility by some colleagues who triggered security inquiries that put them both in danger. They had to flee, for there was nowhere to hide in the country.

Dan followed the path towards Grant Market through the vacant lot on the Dâmbovița shore once called Oatu's Pit. Modest little houses now filled this place, clustered along narrow streets lined with winter-bare trees. Every Sunday, farmers from nearby villages brought their carts, gathering behind the market on the edge of the land with their horses, which they unhitched, blanketed, and tethered with a bundle of hay before them. The market stalls held milk, cream, cheese, butter, and eggs. Some even sold chickens in wire cages or other fowls, goats, or the occasional horse or colt. Dan bought a cube of cheese wrapped in newspaper, a dozen eggs in a worn bag, and some shriveled apples. Cradling the eggs close to his chest to avoid breaking them, he made his way to his aunt's house.

"What's going on, Dănuț, so early in the morning?" asked

his aunt as he entered. "Did something happen?"

"No, Auntie, nothing happened. The factory is sending me to some collective farms that need spare parts for their machines."

His aunt, in her nightgown with a robe fastened around her middle, was tying her long, waist-length white hair into a skillful bun at the back. At almost sixty, she was still as beautiful and agile as she'd been in her youth.

"Why would they send you? You're no mechanic."

"I don't know. They couldn't find anyone else. I've no wife or kids..."

"But where are these parts?"

"In a box at the station. I left them there yesterday until the train leaves."

"And where are you headed?"

"Moldova, near Focșani."

"Do you have time to eat something? Shall I make some sandwiches for the road?"

"Here, I brought eggs, cheese, and apples from the market."

"Good idea! I have some fried pork cracklings and smoked bacon from your father. How long will you be staying?"

"I'm not sure. They didn't say. I think I should pack a few

changes of clothes in case it's longer."

"Yes, take some thick socks for the cold and a jacket to keep you warm. But where are you off to now?" she asked, seeing him head for the door.

"I'll chop some firewood for when I'm gone..."

"Wouldn't you like to eat first? I'll warm the milk…"

"I'll eat later," Dan said, closing the door.

The woodshed was in the backyard, a dark, windowless place with dirt floors and a row of logs stacked from the summer rations. Some logs were there from ages, harder to split. There were a couple of sacks of coal, and at the far end, by the wall, a barrel of pickled cabbage and some jars of preserves on a shelf. Dan took off his jacket, grabbed a stubborn log, and placed it on the solid stump used for splitting. He raised the ax over his head and brought it down hard on the log.

He pitied his aunt. He knew she would shed many tears when he was gone, not knowing where he wandered or even if he was still alive. He felt for his father, left alone and aging without support, but what could he do? Telling them what he intended would only put himself and Rozica in even greater danger. And they would face the torment of keeping a secret to protect him while being hounded by security officers, forced to write statements, and threatened with accusations of betrayal if they didn't confess. This agony could stretch into hours and days of harrowing interrogations, promises that if they told the truth, their suffering, and his, would be lessened, and a judge might overlook his complicity in Anișoara's death.

"Yes, that's why they're after me: Anișoara's death. Though I know I'm blameless, the fact that I was the last person she spoke to before dying gives them a powerful reason to accuse me."

Sweat began to bead on Dan's forehead, though the woodshed was cold with the door open. Driven by fury, he brought the ax down relentlessly on the stubborn logs in front of him as if he were taking revenge on them for the injustice pursuing him. Around him grew a pile of split wood, which he kicked aside to make room for another log and then another. After finishing the last one, he took an armful of firewood into the kitchen and stacked it under the stove. Then he went back for another load.

Standing in the kitchen, his aunt busily prepared sandwiches, watching him from the corner of her eye as he moved with the practiced hand of a man who knew his way around things.

"He's grown up, that lucky boy, tall and handsome, a hard-working lad just like his father was in his youth," she thought.

She was filled with motherly pride, seeing how hard he tried to help without having to be asked. After they shared a meal of fried eggs and a mug of milk, Dan gathered several sets of clothes from his aunt's wardrobe and stuffed them into a backpack. Then he emptied his uncle's wartime gas mask bag, brought it into the kitchen, and placed his aunt's sandwiches, which she wrapped in a cloth. He was ready to go, with plans to meet Rozica at the railway station.

A terrible tenderness washed over him, bringing tears to his eyes. This was no ordinary parting; it was a final departure, and only he knew it. He was leaving behind everything dear to him: his parents, his aunt, who stood waiting for his farewell kiss, his home, his friends, and the country of his birth. Struggling to keep his composure, he slung his sack over his shoulder, shook his hands out, unsure what to say, and embraced his aunt, kissing her on both cheeks.

"Goodbye, Auntie!"

"Go with God, Dănuț! May the Holy Mother keep you safe!"

"Bless you!" Dan replied, kissing her once more.

As he left the yard, he paused in the street to look one last time at the house of the aunt who had been like a mother to him.

"God, watch over all that I leave behind," Dan prayed. "Have mercy on them and on us all! Amen."

He crossed and headed toward the station.

David Kimel

# **The Departure**

Gara de Nord (The North Railway Station), teeming with people, seemed like a city by itself. Thousands of travelers traversed their waiting rooms, ticket counters, and the platforms aligned with ten railway tracks behind iron-grilled barriers with panels indicating the direction and departure time of each train. From there, hundreds of trains set off toward various corners of the country and beyond its borders. Entering from Calea Griviței into the third-class waiting room, Dan glanced up at the large, round clock that hung above the door leading to the trains. It was a quarter to twelve. He stopped at one of the many ticket counters and asked where he could buy the train schedule book. The cashier handed him a booklet. With the booklet in hand, Dan headed toward the information desk on the platform, expecting to meet Rozica. She hadn't yet arrived. Dan circled the information booth in the center of the platform, trying to spot the girl's familiar face among the swarming travelers who moved in every direction. Meanwhile, a young boy circled him like an annoying mosquito. He wore baggy pants, a mountaineer's jacket, a military rucksack, and a cap that was too large for his head. Dan turned sharply to scold him, but, catching a glimpse of the boy's face, he stopped, recognizing Rozica's smiling eyes. He hadn't imagined she could undergo such a transformation and, instead of scolding her, realized the wisdom of her disguise. He said jokingly:

"Young man, if you're coming with me, you'll have to listen to everything I say!"

"Yes, sir," Rozica replied.

"Remind me, what's your name?"

"Lion's fame…"

"No, seriously, you must have a name…"

"Rob. Would Robert do?"

"Hmm, but wouldn't it be easier if I called you Radu or Rică?"

"Rică? Rică fără frică (the fearless)?"

"Yes. How's that?"

"Sound's good."

From a distance, they looked like two friends of different ages. One older, a man from the countryside who could pass for a city dweller in his sturdy woolen coat and lambskin hat covering his forehead; the other, a young city boy, barely old enough to grow a mustache, or perhaps one that was too light to be seen. Dan now noticed that her beautiful golden hair, which used to cascade over her shoulders and back, had been cut short, boyishly hidden under the checkered cap. The sight opened a wound in Dan's heart, a painful regret he couldn't hide. Sensing the shadow of sorrow in his eyes, Rozica reassured him that he shouldn't worry; it would grow back soon enough.

"What made you think of dressing up like this?" he asked her.

"I went to one of my father's relatives, who has two boys. My aunt, when she heard what I was planning, advised me to take on a boy's appearance if I wanted to stay safe. She helped me cut my hair."

"So, from now on, will you always be dressed like a boy?"

Rozica shrugged.

"And what would you do if a girl falls in love with you?" Dan asked jokingly.

"Love," she said mischievously. Then she continued, "I think we should move somewhere quieter to figure out where we're going."

Dan looked around for a suitable place, but people were everywhere. Perhaps if they went to the third-class waiting room, they could find a bench where they could sit and browse the train schedule; the ticket counters were there, too. Rozica didn't object. Strangely, both looked around carefully as they walked, watching who they passed and, especially, if anyone seemed to be following them. They found a spot by the wall and sat together on a sturdy oak bench. Dan took the schedule book from his pocket.

"We need to head to the northern part of the country. Wouldn't it be better to start by going west? I told my aunt I was leaving for Moldova, and I don't want to walk straight into the wolf's mouth."

"The west? Timisoara, Arad, and the Danube region are the most dangerous. The border guards have orders to shoot anyone suspicious."

"No, I was thinking of going to Craiova and changing direction from there," Dan said.

Rozica found the idea reasonable. They found a local train that would leave the station in about an hour.

"Now we need to separate, my dear. We won't buy tickets together. We need to stay apart. I'll always be near you, but not as if we know each other. Do you understand?"

Dan nodded bitterly. He didn't want to reveal his anxiety about traveling into the unknown, mingling among a haphazard crowd of people, each with their own intentions and behaviors. It was hard to resist the pressure of constant movement, frustration, and agitation created by the crowd. He wanted to stay close to her, to protect her with his strength, ready to fend off those who pushed their way through. Sensing they might face challenges on the train, he longed to keep her nearby.

Rozica let Dan go to the ticket counter first while she approached the next window. With tickets in hand, they walked one behind the other to the platform on the fourth line, where the Craiova train was due. They sat on the same bench but at opposite ends. Rozica pulled the hood of her gray canvas jacket over her cap as the cold draft was freezing her ears. Porters pushed carts loaded with crates and packages past them toward the end of the platform. Behind them, many travelers with suitcases or bags began to spread across the yellowish ceramic pavement shaded by the steel roof raised on iron pillars above the wagons' roof. A row of passenger cars slowly rolled onto their platform, inching forward on the tracks until it came to a complete stop.

Dan didn't hurry to board the third-class car in front of him, and Rozica waited to see what he would do. Most travelers jostled to grab better spots by the windows in cars with wooden benches lined up on either side of the corridor linking the two entrance doors in the middle. Only a few passengers headed for the more luxurious second or first-class cars. When the commotion subsided, Rozica moved toward the right-hand staircase of the car in front of them and found a seat on the edge of a bench near the door leading to other cars. Dan did the same at the opposite end of the car, where he could keep an eye on her. Ten minutes later, the train began moving, leaving behind only a few handkerchiefs waving in the air. Crossing himself, Dan whispered a prayer in his mind.

"God help us! Who knows if I'll ever come this way again," Dan thought at last.

From the other end of the car, reading his thoughts, Rozica nodded encouragingly as if to assure him:

"Yes, dear. We will succeed, and we'll come back!"

David Kimel

# On the Road

With the train schedule book in hand, Dan estimated that the journey to Satu Mare could take between 16 and 20 hours if traveled continuously on a direct route. In their case, however, it could take two or three days. This was undoubtedly going to be complicated, he thought, especially considering his separation from Rozica. If only they could stay together, they could better plan what to do, and it might have been possible for them to take turns dozing under one another's watchful eye. But as it was, he felt exposed to unpredictable situations, surrounded by strangers with unknown intentions. This thought made Dan stand up, take the bag off his shoulders, and place it on the rack above his head. Standing, he could see over the heads of those standing and take stock of who Rozica had around her as traveling companions. Most of the passengers in the carriage were men of various ages: villagers from nearby communes who had come to the capital on business, peasants with their wives, sacks and woven reed or wicker baskets, workers going to see their families for a few hours on the weekend, and even a few children. Some wore city coats and carried polished leather bags.

Across from Rozica sat a woman with a little girl and her husband. He was showing the child the landscape as the train passed through, trying to wipe the frosty window with the sleeve of his coat. The carriage wasn't heated, and many people were tapping their feet to keep from freezing. Both the mother and the girl wore their heads wrapped in floral cotton scarves, with woolen shawls draped over their shoulders. Next to Rozica sat a peasant with a shaggy hat and sheepskin coat, holding a sack on his knees, and at the window, a middle-aged man with glasses and a hat. Reassured, Dan returned to his seat next to a man who was trying to start a conversation with the young woman by the window. When he offered her a cigarette, she declined, saying she didn't smoke. The man then offered the pack to Dan.

"Thanks, but I don't smoke either," Dan replied politely.

The man lit his own cigarette and put the pack back in his pocket.

"Are you going far?" he asked.

"To Craiova."

"Do you live there?"

Dan preferred not to get into conversations with those around him, and to ward off his nosy neighbor; he whispered a little mysteriously:

"I have a UTM (The Young Workers Union) assignment I can't talk about," he said.

The man seemed to understand, turning back to the young woman beside him with other questions, which pleased Dan. Through the crowd, the train conductor appeared to punch the travelers' tickets. A passenger in front of Dan apologized, saying he hadn't had time to buy a ticket at the counter, and asked the conductor if he could sell him one.

"To where?" asked the conductor.

"To Videle," the man replied. "My godfather's niece is getting married, and I have to be there."

Everyone smiled, glancing sympathetically at the man who was heading to a celebration. The person next to him, an elderly villager with gray hair covering his ears and a mustache, pulled a bottle of brandy from the bag on the floor between his feet and said:

"Well then, let's drink to the groom and bride!"

He took the first swig, then handed the bottle to the young weddinggoer, who, after taking a sip, passed it to the conductor.

"No, I can't; I'm on duty," the conductor politely declined.

"Oh, come on, you're among friends here," said the villager. "Take a sip for the bride's good fortune!"

The conductor took a sip, then wiped his lips with the back of his hand and returned the bottle. The villager handed it to Dan, who took a drink before passing it to the next person.

"To your health!"

"Thanks!"

The train stopped at almost every village halt. Some passengers got off, others boarded, and the conductor made sure to announce the next station's stop through the carriages. Many took out what food they had, and Dan retrieved his bag from the rack and went over to where Rozica was sitting. She noticed him and understood he wanted to speak with her. She grabbed her backpack from the rack and stepped out onto the platform at the end of the car. He followed her. There were also people waiting to get off at the next station, but she stopped by the passage to the next car.

"Aren't you hungry? I've got some sandwiches in my bag. Do you want one?" Dan asked.

"I have some from my aunt," Rozica replied.

"Are you tired? Maybe it would be better if we sat together; it's getting late, and it's not good to be separated."

"Not yet. It's too risky. When I feel myself starting to get sleepy, I'll eat something or stand up..."

"For how long? You didn't sleep last night either, did you?"

Rozica looked at his face, darkened by worry. She didn't know what to say. She had her own doubts, for which she found no answers. All she knew was that, at that moment, one of them had to be strong and resist weakness because they had no other choice. She touched his tense hand on the railing and returned to her seat in the car. Dan lingered for a while on the front platform. When he re-entered the car, his seat was occupied. He stopped halfway through the carriage, standing in the aisle that separated the rows of benches. Rozica now had different people around her. The family with the little girl was gone, as was the peasant next to her. Only the man with the hat by the window remained in his seat. Rozica sat next to him.

The train continued to pass through wooded areas and fields blanketed with snow under the gray evening sky, stopping in front of small, whitewashed buildings the stations of the communes through which the line ran. A few electric lamps suspended from the ceiling above the aisle lit up the car. When the conductor announced the next station, Caracal, Rozica stood up and stepped out onto the platform.

"What's going on?" Dan asked as he joined her on the platform.

"We're getting off here."

"Why?"

"That creep next to me has a taste for young boys."

"How do you know?"

"He invited me to go with him to the restroom." Dan laughed.

"And what did you say to him?"

"That I wasn't interested."

"Did he understand?"

"No. He kept trying to convince me I'd feel great afterward, that I shouldn't have a preconceived notion about something as normal as that..."

"And that's why you want to get off here?"

"Yes. I think it's better. We might even find a more direct train."

Dan thought of checking the schedule from his pocket, but it was too dark on the platform. At that moment, "the creep," the man with the hat who'd been next to Rozica, stepped out onto the platform. Seeing Rozica talking with Dan, he hesitated, unsure whether to approach her or not. Dan positioned himself between them with a hard stare. The man then opened the restroom door and stepped inside.

When they got off the train at Caracal, Dan pulled Rozica to the edge of the platform, letting the crowd of people spill out of the station or head toward the carriages that had stopped at the station. When the bustle in the station quieted down, they entered the waiting room and sat on a bench side by side. Exhaustion began to show on their faces. Rozica pulled her hood over the cap on her head and closed her eyes. Dan leafed through the train schedule and moved closer to the ticket window, where there was lighter, and he could read. The man behind the window opened the small pane and asked:

"Where are you headed?"

"Well, I just want to see what connections I have here," Dan replied.

"Tell me where you want to go, and I'll tell you the connections."

"Well, let's see, to Târgu-Mureş..."

"You'll have to change trains at Sibiu. Want me to sell you a ticket to Târgu-Mureş?"

"When's the next train to Sibiu?"

"At ten, in about two hours..."

"All right. I'll talk to my friend first, and then I'll get the tickets."

The cashier pulled the glass pane closed again. Dan returned to the bench at the back of the waiting room, where Rozica was waiting for him. They were the only ones in the room. With her elbow propped on the armrest, Rozica had dozed off, her head leaning on her cupped palm. Dan opened the schedule to the map of rail routes and was finally able to see what options they had. Sibiu was the best direction. Seated beside her, he, too, dozed off.

David Kimel

# The Amber-Handled Knife

When Dan opened his eyes, the waiting room was buzzing with the activity that always preceded the arrival of the train to Sibiu. Rozica was no longer by his side on the bench, and, surprised, he scanned the room for her among the bustling crowd. He got up to check if she had gone out to the platform, but when he re-entered the waiting area, he saw her coming from the opposite direction.

"Where did you go?" asked Dan.

"Where even the emperor goes…" she replied.

"To the men's or the women's?"

"If I'd gone to the women's, the ladies would've beaten me up."

"You should've gone with me—you never know what sort of creep might show up…"

Rozica didn't respond to Dan's suggestion. Instead, he stopped at the ticket window.

"Two third-class tickets to Sibiu."

The man behind the window asked, "Didn't you say you wanted to go to Târgu-Mureş?"

"Yes," Dan replied, "but I have a friend in Sibiu I haven't seen in ages, and I thought I'd stop by to see him first."

After getting their tickets, they went out to the small platform where the train to Sibiu would soon arrive. They weren't alone there. Blackened remnants of snow, mixed with coarse salt, covered the stone slabs of the platform. The dim light of a few lanterns hung from the station walls allowed them to make out the faces of other travelers. They were relieved that no one was paying them any attention, though their main fear was that they might be followed. They anticipated that early in the morning when people at the factory realized neither of them had shown up, a real search would be underway; telegraph services would be dispatching their photographs everywhere, and security agents would be tasked with finding them. Rozica's disguise as a young man and their early disembarkation at Caracal with tickets marked for Craiova seemed like a wise choice.

When the train arrived, they boarded one of the first carriages behind the locomotive, finding seats next to each other on the same bench. During the night journey to Sibiu, they could still sit side by side. Opposite them, three soldiers occupied the bench, a sergeant with a soldier, and between them, a young man in military uniform, without shoulder boards or a belt, with handcuffs on his wrists. The detainee's face was pale, looking both worried and embarrassed that people could see him in such a state. He kept his head down, his gaze fixed on the carriage floor. The seat by the window next to Rozica was taken by a priest with a beard and hair graying from age.

As Dan stood to place Rozica's military rucksack on the luggage rack, the priest observed the newcomers beside him and, to excuse his scrutiny, asked if school vacation had started earlier that year.

"No," Rozica replied, her cheeks flushed with redness, understanding that she'd been mistaken for a schoolboy. "Vacation is later, but my cousin and I visited a sick uncle who was alone."

"I see," said the priest, nodding. "How is he doing now, left by himself?"

"My cousin and I helped him get into the hospital in Caracal."

"Well done, my child, you did a good deed," said the priest.

The detainee sitting across from them requested to go to the restroom, and the soldier accompanied him. The sergeant left on the bench, pulled a cigarette from the pocket of his uniform when the priest addressed him, curious:

"What did your comrade do?"

"He refused to take the military oath."

"Why, son?"

"He says his faith won't let him kill…"

"What sort of faith does he follow?"

"He's a believer… one of those sects, I think… He was convicted by the Military Tribunal."

"What are you telling, son? Just for that?"

"Well, you see, military service is mandatory. Anyone who refuses the oath is considered a traitor."

The priest fell silent, lost in thought until the detainee was brought back to his seat. This time, the priest's gaze lingered on the young man with handcuffed hands.

"I heard you refused to take the oath. Why?"

"Well, the Lord commanded that we shall not kill. I cannot kill another human being. That's why I…"

The clergyman struggled to find words to respond to this young man who would be imprisoned for his beliefs. His experience taught him that it was wise to say no more than necessary. After some quiet contemplation, he finally said to the young man,

"The Lord be with you, my son."

"Kiss your hand, Father!"

By now, it was late at night, and each person tried to find a comfortable position to get a bit of sleep. Rozica asked Dan to pass her the rucksack from the luggage rack. Standing up, Dan handed her the military backpack, from which she took out a vividly red Jonathan apple. After giving the rucksack back to Dan, Rozica pulled a small pocketknife from her coat, its blade hidden in an amber handle. Opening the blade, she sliced the apple in half and handed one to Dan. As she moved to put the pocketknife back in her pocket, the priest asked if he might have a look at the beautiful tool. Surprised, Rozica handed the knife to the man next to her. The priest examined it carefully on both sides, then drew a fine silver toothpick hidden in the amber handle.

"Where did you get this knife?"

"It's been in my family for a long time, as long as I can remember…"

"Do you see this emblem here with the crown and shield engraved on the handle?"

Rozica turned the knife over and, for the first time, noticed the symbols the priest had pointed out. She hadn't known about the hidden silver toothpick either, which the priest had discovered.

"What does it mean?" she asked.

"It belonged to a noble family from the past."

"Which family?"

"To my family," the priest whispered after making sure no one was listening. "That's why I want to know how it ended up with you."

"I don't know," replied Rozica. "It's always been in our house. My mother kept it in her purse."

"Your mother? What was her name?"

"Sima," Rozica replied, her cheeks flushed. She didn't want to reveal that her real name was Simha, which in Hebrew means "joy."

"Sima? Long ago, in my youth, I met a girl. Her name was different, Simha…"

Rozica was stunned to hear the priest say her mother's name. This encounter felt unreal. It was extraordinary to meet a stranger on a train, a priest no less, who had known her mother years ago.

"What happened to that girl?" Rozica asked.

"It's a long story," the priest replied, lost in nostalgic memory. "We were classmates at the conservatory. She was very beautiful and had a voice like no other. I fell madly in love with her at first sight. But we couldn't marry because she was…" The priest stopped, looking intently at the passenger beside him.

"Wait a moment; your mother was a well-known artist before the war. She sang in operettas, didn't she?"

Rozica nodded before realizing that this confirmation might reveal her identity. This man could almost have been her father, she thought, though she knew she had been born a year after her parents married.

"As far as I know, she married a journalist and had a daughter," the priest continued his gaze still on Rozica, whose face reddened all at once.

He noted her delicate, sensual features, her feminine grace, so similar to his former love. Her slender figure, mannerisms, and well-kept, long, thin fingers betrayed her gender. Now, the priest began to suspect that there was a mystery behind this girl's disguise. He decided it was best to remain discreet, avoiding probing into the reasons for her attire.

"Tell me, what happened to Simha, your mother? Is she still alive?"

"No," the girl whispered.

"Sorry! I loved her deeply, but I wasn't permitted to marry her. Because of her, I chose the path of the church. I was naïve. I thought I could change people's mentality, but it wasn't possible. The evils of the Unholy One are strong, and people are not worthy of following the way of reason."

Looking at the little knife in the girl's hands, the priest began murmuring his memories to himself. Years ago, after a singing lesson at the conservatory, he had gone with Simha to the

Oteleleşanu Terrace on Calea Victoriei, near the National Theater. They sat at a table beneath the shadow of three large chestnut trees, savoring steaming cups of coffee. At that time, nougat was a fashionable treat, and ordering some, he had taken the small knife from his vest pocket to cut the nougat into small, easy-to-chew pieces. Simha had admired the amber-handled tool, and he had insisted that she keep it. Coming out of his reverie, the priest smiled and said,

"Thank you. You've helped me remember things long forgotten, as if from another life, with other people and places. Today, where the Oteleleşanu Terrace once stood, now stands the Telephone Palace. The National Theater was destroyed by German bombings, and since then, everything is different."

"What's your name?" Rozica asked.

"I am now Father Ştefan Suţu."

Noticing her inquisitive look, the priest continued,

"My ancestors were rulers of Wallachia. But it's late now; maybe there's still time for a short nap before we reach our destination."

However, Rozica couldn't fall asleep after this conversation. She'd never known her mother had a love story before marrying her father. This man beside her had guessed who she was without forcing her into any unpleasant admissions, showing her that he was someone she could trust and respect. It was a shame to have met him only now when a future meeting would be impossible. Such a shame.

Meanwhile, Dan, seated on the aisle side of the bench, watched what was happening in their carriage, holding the travel bag on his lap, along with the sandwich bag his aunt had prepared. After a while, he pulled the train timetable from his coat pocket to check the connections from Sibiu to Satu Mare. First, they had to reach Alba Iulia to catch the train to Cluj. The next train to Alba Iulia was around 10 in the morning, so they would have time to spend in Sibiu before continuing. Feeling tired, he rested his arms across the bag on his lap and, laying his head on them, immediately fell asleep. Rozica leaned her head on his shoulder, and soon she, too, drifted off.

# Simha

After his conversation with Rozica, the priest couldn't sleep, though he dearly wished to rest enough to function the next morning without feeling worn from the journey. He lay with his eyes closed for a while until, at one of the stops, the three soldiers disembarked. When new passengers took their seats, he realized sleep was elusive and began observing his surroundings. The new arrivals, ordinary people traveling for their own purposes, sought a more comfortable position on the immovable wooden bench. They brought with them the chilly outdoor air, tinged with the smell of coarse tobacco and a hint of brandy. After the conductor punched their tickets, a quiet settled over the carriage, broken only by the rhythmic clatter of the wheels on the tracks, like the ticking of a clock.

From his corner, leaning against the window frame, the priest observed the bodies around him, huddled from the cold and exhaustion. Beside him, barely touching his knee, was the girl dressed as a boy, concealing a mysterious secret. Next to her was the young man, doing everything he could to protect her, a friend, or perhaps a lover, aware of her secret and willing to comply, even at the risk of undertaking acts condemned by law. She seemed no older than twenty, maybe not even that. Her entire appearance, especially her eyes and smile, brought to life the image of someone who, in his own youth, had embodied divine perfection. How many people could say that their destiny had been entirely altered by the arrival of a woman, of a love that was not meant to be? Not many, he thought. Some might argue that their fate had taken an unwanted turn, but how many would admit that because of love, all their plans were shattered? In his case, it was not only possible but true.

When he met Simha, Ștefan Suțu was with a group of friends at a matinée at the Cărăbuș Theatre on Calea Victoriei. The star of the show was the famous black artist Josephine Baker, brought from Paris for an entire season by the theatre director Constantin Tănase. The excitement around this great artist only intensified when, after arriving in the capital with the Orient Express train, she drove a small carriage drawn by an ostrich from the train station to her hotel. Curious onlookers, who had never seen anything like it, followed her every step. Evening newspapers covered the event with reports, photos, and statements from amazed passers-by about this extravagant display by the Folies Bergère star. On another occasion, she entered the Capșa confectionery alone, dressed in men's trousers, leaving the mostly male audience with mouths agape. It wasn't common then for a woman to enter a café alone, much less in pants. The surprise, whispers, and comments created quite a stir in the city, and her show tickets, although expensive, became hard to obtain even for those with connections.

Before the show began, a family with two elderly people and a very beautiful young lady appeared in the row in front of Ștefan.

Dressed in a simple, unadorned dress, she had blue eyes, straw-colored hair, and a wasp-like waist. Ștefan couldn't take his eyes off this girl, who was likely accompanied by her parents. His friends noticed his attraction and began teasing him loudly. Annoyed, Ștefan warned them that if they didn't stop immediately, he would end his friendship with them. At that moment, the girl turned her head to see who was sitting behind her. Taken by surprise, he smiled at her, and she quickly turned back to face the stage. When the curtain rose, Ștefan, lost in thoughts of her and how he might get to know her, missed what happened on stage during the first part of the show.

He decided that, during the intermission, he would pass her a note requesting a meeting. Taking a pen from his pocket, he tore a page from his notebook, where he jotted down important notes, and wrote a few words, carefully folding the note and placing it in his buttonhole pocket. When the curtain fell for intermission, he rushed out to the theater's main hall to wait for the girl to appear. But she didn't show up. Instead, he spotted her parents approaching the hall, her distinguished father adjusting a cigarette in his holder and lighting it. Realizing that the girl was still inside, Ștefan returned to his seat and, from a distance, saw her reading intently the program. Back in his seat behind the girl, he pretended to pick something up from the floor, but suddenly, the gesture felt silly, and he put the note back in his pocket. Standing behind her, he asked:

"Pardon me for asking, but would the commentary in the program not influence your personal opinion of the show?"

"Why do you ask?" she replied, looking up at him.

"Out of curiosity. I, for one, refuse to read what's written in the program or critics' reviews, which are often paid for their praise. At least my opinion is sincere and impartial…"

"But it could also be wrong," she noted, blushing.

"I don't deny it. I don't claim to be a good judge in the field of art, but I can try to be honest."

"In what field do you consider yourself a good judge?"

At this, Ştefan was taken aback and couldn't find an immediate answer. He stammered, then finally admitted resignedly:

"To be honest, none… I'm a law student. My name is Ştefan Suţu. I noticed you when you entered the hall and wanted to meet you. Could you tell me your name?"

"Simha," she replied, smiling at him.

"May I see you again?"

"I don't know. Maybe. My schedule is very busy…"

"Busy? With what?"

"With studying. I'm a music student at the conservatory, studying voice. My teacher is very strict and thorough."

"Who are you studying with?"

"With Madam Stănculescu."

"May I wait for you after your class one evening?"

"Can I stop you?"

"I'm afraid not…" he said, smiling.

At that moment, the intermission ended, people began to reclaim their seats, and Simha's parents reappeared to resume their seats. Stefan's friends were equally surprised to see him talking to the young woman. Before her parents sat down, Simha introduced the young man she had been speaking with:

"This is Mr. Ștefan Suțu…"

Her father extended his hand cordially.

"Dr. Horovici."

"Pleased to meet you."

After this brief introduction to the Horovici family, Ștefan, who was gifted with a lovely baritone voice, thought it wouldn't be a bad idea to enroll in the Conservatory for singing lessons. With the help of a relative, he arranged an audience with the Conservatory's director, Mr. Ion Nonna Otescu, a prominent composer and promoter of Romanian musical education, who granted his request to take singing lessons. Now, colleagues of the same institution would have the chance to see Simha almost daily.

The more he got to know her, the more Ștefan felt that his attraction to this girl was of a different kind than any previous relationship. He was surprised by the depth of her thoughts, resistant to superficiality and immune to flattery and easy praise. She was full of grace, a love for beauty, and a disarming innocence. Every moment spent with her was miraculously beautiful, and each farewell came with the regret that their time together was too short. He felt he was in love with Simha, and this realization couldn't be ignored.

Worried that love could blind him, Ștefan began to bring Simha to some social gatherings frequented by notable personalities from the art world. Wherever she appeared with Ștefan, the young woman radiated beauty, simplicity, and intelligence. Her presence was increasingly appreciated and even sought after by acquaintances. Ștefan suddenly found himself more respected by friends who showed a clear attraction to Simha. However, she didn't seem impressed by the influential figures she met, which left Ștefan feeling disarmed. He believed she would be grateful for the opportunities he offered, but Simha did not act as though he had done anything extraordinary. Wanting to prove his social standing, Ștefan strove to secure an invitation to the Palace for one of King Carol II's receptions following his return to the country. That evening, the King himself approached and requested permission to dance with the beautiful young woman. After the dance ended, Carol kept Simha aside from the orchestra, offering her a glass of champagne. The King held a brief, charming conversation with her before returning her to Ștefan. The attention from the King flattered Ștefan, who hadn't anticipated that the monarch would hold him in such high regard. After the reception, as he walked her to her parents' house, Simha told Ștefan that the King had proposed a secret meeting, which she declined by claiming she was engaged to Ștefan. Only then did Ștefan understand why, upon returning with Simha, the King had congratulated him, holding his shoulder warmly and wishing him lasting happiness and prosperity.

The train continued its monotonous journey through the snow-covered mountain passes, stopping occasionally at small provincial stations. Some passengers boarded, others disembarked, and the journey continued as before, with the shrill whistle sounding at each crossing. Rozica woke up after a while, glanced around, wiping the sleep from her eyes, then spotted the priest next to her, smiled faintly, and rose to step outside. Returning after a few moments, she smiled again, sat back down on the bench, and, glancing at her wristwatch, said:

"Morning is almost here."

"Yes, you still have a little time to sleep before we arrive."

David Kimel

# Mihai Cută

The rumor of Ștefan's engagement to Simha spread quickly among their circle of friends, amusing the couple at first as though it were an inside joke known only to the two of them. But soon enough, their family members, alarmed by what they'd heard from others, began questioning them with pointed questions. It was one thing, Ștefan's family said, for him to have a relationship with a beautiful "Jewess," but quite another to marry her. At first, Ștefan tried to calm his family's concerns by saying they weren't engaged and that it had merely been an excuse in front of the sovereign. Seeing that no one believed him, he eventually, exasperated, declared that regardless, he would marry Simha because it wasn't her fault she was born Jewish, and she was nothing like the others.

Similarly, Simha had to confess to her parents that she was in love with Ștefan, her devoted and sincere friend, with whom she felt understood and who believed in her artistic potential. Hearing this, the entire Horovici family, not only Simha's father, launched a full campaign to find a suitable candidate, equal to her in worth and age, for her to marry. Out of the many selected, they settled on a young, well-known journalist from a respectable family, an intellectual and editor at 'Adevărul' (The Truth), whose editorials were widely appreciated by readers. Despite Simha's protests, who did not want to hear what they planned, she met Mordechai Tenenbaum at a party organized by a cousin with many young people. Mordechai, whom everyone called Mişu but who signed his articles with the pseudonym Mihai Cută (Mihai with T for Tenenbaum), as at that time, Jewish intellectuals were less tolerated by the public, especially in the press, was advised to use a pseudonym.

After dancing with Simha, Mişu asked if she'd like to join him on the terrace for some fresh air while he smoked a cigarette. They talked for a long time under the silver light of the moon. He was a tall man with an athletic build, dark eyes, and black hair, giving him an oriental look. A keen observer of everything around him with a sense of humor, he conversed with ease without trying to dominate the discussion. She immediately liked Mişu, admiring his knowledge and courtesy. At the end of the soirée, Mişu asked if he might visit her sometime. She felt it would be impolite to say no.

Meanwhile, Ştefan fought fiercely with his own family, especially his father, who was furious and swore "on the cross," as he said, that he would disinherit Ştefan if he married Simha. Hearing this, Ştefan retorted that he would give up his family name and his family if they disrespected his wishes. If he couldn't marry Simha, he'd go join a monastery or take his own life.

Neither of them was in a good situation. Realizing Ştefan's

dilemma, Simha felt guilty for his suffering. Since she was equally distressed, she told Ştefan one evening that it might be best to part ways and thus spare their families the pain. Ştefan refused to listen to any such argument, insisting that their love must prevail. After weeks of sorrow, overwhelmed by unsolvable dilemmas, with a heart broken by futile struggles, she confessed one day that she had decided to accept Mişu's proposal. Ştefan could hardly believe what he was hearing, as he knew how deeply she loved him, how out of love for him, she'd agreed, after much hesitation, to sacrifice her chastity, and for that reason, he couldn't understand how she could now utter such words.

In the meantime, Simha made her debut in a concert on the Opera House stage, performed by the Conservatory's most talented members. The success of this concert was undeniably immense and marked the remarkable careers of several protagonists. Simha, young and beautiful, with a striking stage presence and a crystal-clear voice, received numerous offers from prominent producers, with the most promising one coming from an operetta company that offered her the role of Adele in "Die Fledermaus" by Johann Strauss. On the evening of her premiere, Ştefan encountered Mişu in her dressing room. They greeted each other politely but awkwardly. Neither felt comfortable in the other's presence and Simha, noticing the tension between them, asked them to return to their seats.

Mişu had been aware of her relationship with Ştefan from

the beginning, as Simha had confided in him once their friendship grew. He knew enough of Ștefan's past, which many regarded as a series of fleeting affairs among the many beautiful women of the capital. It seemed his prowess had calmed down after meeting Simha. Now, however, faced with Ștefan, who looked as sullen as someone who had bet everything on a horse that lost the race, while Mișu, confident and self-possessed, appeared to be in control of the situation. They left Simha in silence, and as they entered the hall, they took their seats in the same row but apart, waiting for the curtain to rise. After the first act, Ștefan left the theater without explanation or farewell, knowing that his "match" was lost. He went to Capșa, ordered a brandy, and began to contemplate the situation.

He had a plan for revenge: to hurt Simha and everyone else, a sacrifice had to be made, and the person to be sacrificed would be him. There was no other way! This would be his ultimate revenge, and it would make them all regret how they'd treated him. He'd promised to do it, and now the time had come to fulfill it without turning back. He would join a monastery. Let this last act of his serve as a lesson for all times! Like Romeo and Juliet, love should not be shackled by outdated principles, racial or religious!

Now, as he looked at the girl beside him, with her short-cropped hair, disturbed by these memories, Ștefan thought that, in truth, his sacrifice had helped nothing. No one had learned anything from his retreat to a monastery in Moldova. Life continued as usual, and people quickly forgot the price he paid for an impossible love. "Romeo and Juliet" become outdated and is no longer in style. It remained a myth, an ordinary story unnoticed today, as there is nothing to learn from it. Even less from the story of his love.

# The Man of God

With weary eyes, Dan looked around the train compartment, noticing the changes that had occurred while he drifted into sleep. Rozica was still dozing, leaning on his shoulder, and beside her, the priest, with open eyes, smiled at him from his spot by the window. The passengers on the bench across from them were still asleep. Outside, darkness lingered, pierced only by the rumbling of wheels and the occasional shrill whistle of the train as it wound through the mountains. He felt cold, realizing the chill had seeped through the floor, leaving his legs stiff. To loosen them up, he began bouncing on the wooden floor, which woke Rozica.

"Have we arrived?" she asked.

"Not yet. I think it's not much longer," Dan replied.

She sat up, rubbing her eyes. To her right, she saw the priest watching her every movement, smiling in greeting. He stood, stretching his back and putting his hands on his shoulders, then looked at the young couple beside him and asked:

"Are you staying in Sibiu?"

Rozica was caught off guard, didn't know what to answer, and looked at Dan.

"No. We're headed to Alba Iulia," he said.

"But I thought you lived in Bucharest?" the priest asked, looking at Rozica.

Now even more embarrassed, unsure what to say, she lowered her gaze and finally admitted:

"It's complicated…"

Dan, surprised by her response, looked intently at Rozica. The priest noted the girl's discomfort, which only strengthened his suspicion that these young people were going through a challenging time. Filled with compassion, he asked:

"Is there some way I can help?"

Without looking on his eyes, the girl shook her head. Dan continued to study her, confused by her answers, which hinted at the fragility of their plans. Finally, under the weight of his steady gaze, Rozica said:

"The priest knows who I am; he knew my mother… He's an experienced man of God, someone who could help us. I think we can trust him."

At these words, Dan now looked at the priest as though seeing him for the first time. The priest, somewhat embarrassed, resumed his seat on the bench beside Rozica. Meanwhile, the other passengers in the car, sensing the train was nearing its destination, began preparing to disembark.

"I live here in Sibiu," the priest said. "If you like, you could come with me, and we could talk."

Dan and Rozica exchanged a quick, questioning look, after which the girl said that perhaps they could talk with him at the station. The priest nodded understandingly. When the train stopped, the passengers crowded toward the two doors leading to the platforms. Dan and Rozica waited patiently for the hurried crowd to disembark. Reaching the platform first, Dan extended his hand to help Rozica down from the last step, which was quite high compared to the platform level, but she declined. Behind her, the priest disembarked, holding a leather bag in his right hand. Dawn had not yet broken, but a sliver of light had begun filtering through the clouds that covered the sky. They entered the large waiting hall, lined with benches in the center and ticket counters along the sides. The steady movement of people from the platform to the station square created a cold draft in the room, making it an uncomfortable place to linger. Rozica moved toward a more secluded bench, but the priest suggested going to a nearby tavern where they could talk quietly in a corner. Dan let them leave first, but he still felt reluctant, uneasy about this diversion from their plan. Instead of quickly resolving their situation as he had hoped, it now seemed to be unraveling with the involvement of a stranger. How did Rozica think this priest could help them? What could this man of the church do something else than pray for them? He wanted to pull Rozica aside and tell her they didn't need this conversation with the priest, that it would be better to just part ways, but he had a feeling she wouldn't listen. He resigned himself and followed.

The large square in front of the Sibiu train station was bustling, full of people, street vendors, carriages, a few taxis, and trams and buses coming and going in different directions. Across from them, on the far right, the outline of a small church with a tower dominated the space in front of the station. The tavern chosen by the priest had a handful of patrons at the counter, drinking shots of țuică or brandy quickly while glancing out the window, waiting for their tram or bus to arrive. The three of them sat at a more secluded table, and the priest ordered cheese pastries and a glass of milk for each of them.

"What's the trouble?" he asked as he took a seat across from the young couple.

"We want to cross the border," Rozica whispered.

The priest was taken aback, not exactly surprised by what he heard but staring intently at their faces.

"Why?"

"We've been accused of things we didn't do. I think the authorities are already after us. If they catch us, it won't end well."

"What did you do?"

"Nothing. We have powerful enemies who want to harm us. My husband is already imprisoned, serving 15 years in Târgu-Mureș because he was a Zionist. Now they're trying to throw me out of my home, where I was born and which has been nationalized. Dan, my friend, is accused of murder because his former girlfriend took her own life. We have no other choice. Do you see?"

"Why did your girlfriend take her own life?" the priest asked Dan.

"I've never understood," he replied. "I loved her very much. While I was away, she resisted those who were cheating the state by falsifying work norms. One day, they caught her, violated her, and tried to kill her by smashing her head. After she was saved and left the hospital, she poisoned herself."

"How were you involved in all this?"

"I was the last person to speak with her before she took her own life."

"I understand," replied the priest, falling silent, his gaze moving across the young faces before him.

"The house that was taken from you—is it the one in Rosetti Square?" he asked Rozica.

"Yes. Do you know the place?"

"I visited often. Your grandparents, Dr. Horovici and his

wife, were hospitable and often invited me to gatherings with their friends. Your mother enchanted us with her golden voice, and sometimes we would sing together."

"I remember those evenings. I was little then. Later, my grandparents died after they arrested my father during the war. Nothing was the same after that."

"Do you think you can help us somehow?" Dan asked, eager to hear what the priest might offer.

"This is more complicated than I anticipated," he said after a moment of thought. "I will try to ask around through some acquaintances. I might be able to find out about your husband's situation in Târgu-Mureș. I used to know someone who worked at that camp. But it will take time… For now, all I can offer is that you stay here for a few days while I make inquiries…"

"I think it's better for us to continue as we planned," Dan said, turning to Rozica.

"Can you really find something out about my husband?" Rozica asked, ignoring Dan's words.

"As I said, I'll try… I must go there; I can't discuss these matters over the phone."

"Rozica, the delay could cost us! Let's keep moving," Dan insisted.

"Where could we stay here?" Rozica asked the priest.

"In my parish, I have a guest room, but you can't stay together. The church caretaker, the woman who raised me, Nana, could help you with anything you need if you want to stay with me. As for him", the priest said, looking at Dan, "I'll find a host for you."

"I must know what's happening with my husband! I haven't heard anything in three years," Rozica said, looking at Dan. "Maybe I could send him a message, something to encourage him. I must take this opportunity, don't you understand?"

"Do you realize what you're putting at stake?" Dan asked.

"In my place, would you act differently?"

At this question, Dan remembered how deeply he had loved Anişoara, for whom no sacrifice would have been too great. If it had been possible to save her in exchange for his life, he wouldn't have hesitated. His love for Rozica, while sincere and filled with affection, couldn't compare to his first love. She probably felt the same way, he thought. That's why memories of her first love held such importance for her. The priest refrained from intervening in the young couple's distressing conversation. He observed, moved by the depth of their feelings reflected in pleading with looks for understanding. He began cutting pieces of warm cheese pastry with his fork while Dan and Rozica continued to wrestle with their dilemma. When they, too, began eating, the priest asked:

"What are your names?"

"My name is Rozica Șfarț. My husband's name is David, David Șfarț."

"And you?"

"Daniel Cristescu."

"What do you do?"

"I was a technician of norms quota and then, for specific material consumption."

"In that case, here's my proposal," the priest said. "I'll take Rozica to my church, leave her at home, and then come back to take you to the host I'll find for you. Stay here until I return. Is that acceptable?"

"And how will I be able to communicate with Rozica after that?"

"We'll think about that later. There's no time now. We'll do what's best…"

Dan felt a lump form in his throat. The priest's proposal seemed harsh and unyielding. The thought of being separated from Rozica in a strange place, at the mercy of fate with no sense of direction, felt like an unexpected blow, leaving him unaccustomed to being out of control, utterly shaken.

"No, Father!" he said, standing up, his tone indignant. "Our plans don't fit with what you're suggesting. We can't be separated, one going one way and the other another."

"Sit down, and don't make a spectacle here. I am known and respected in these parts. Do you forget the situation you're in? Who else can offer you a better solution? Come on! Thank the Lord that I'm willing to help!"

"But we can't be separated," Dan said, feeling tears start to well up. "We set out together with a plan, and we need to be together. Not in the guest room you have. I can stay anywhere, in a shed, a stable over a handful of straw, any place. Rozica and I need to figure out what we're going to do; this situation doesn't allow us to be separated. Rozica, do you want to be separated from me? Can you give up on what we planned?"

"I don't know, Dan. I'm exhausted and don't know anything anymore… The Father is a man of God and wants to help us. What else can we hope for? I think the Lord decided this, and we must leave it in His hands…"

Dan buried his forehead in his hand over the plate before him. He felt the ground slipping out from under him. As if caught in a trap, all his attempts to free himself seemed futile. Rozica, he realized, had abandoned the plan, letting herself be swayed by the promises of this priest, who had no clear way of helping. Crossing the border into Hungary, while the Russians had yet to occupy the entire country after the revolution, might only be possible for a limited number of hours or days. Time was precious, and there was no time to waste. But she couldn't seem to understand that. Dan felt disarmed and powerless in the face of the situation. He could leave on his own, but loyalty kept him from making that choice; without him, who knew what would happen to Rozica? Desperate to find a better argument, he tried once more to sway the priest:

"You know, I can do anything. Any kind of work, hard or easy. I can repair broken things, I can help you with anything you need at the church or at home, and in this way, I can repay you somehow for what you're doing for us. All I ask is that we be together."

"The Church doesn't allow cohabitation out of wedlock! Understand? That's why you can't be together. It goes against our faith, and I won't allow it! Rozica, are you coming with me or not?" the priest said, getting up to pay the bill. Rozica rose, ready to follow, saying to Dan as she passed:

"Don't be upset. He's a serious man who wants to help us. You'll see, it'll be all right."

Returning to the table, the priest touched Dan's shoulder, saying he'd come back in an hour or two to pick him up. Left alone, Dan watched them leave, resigned, as they stepped out into the street.

## The Chapel of the Cross

Shaken by the events of that morning, Dan paused for a moment to gather himself, then, as if jolted awake from a deep sleep, sprang up and hurriedly followed the priest and Rozica. He couldn't leave her without knowing exactly where she was, and he decided he must follow them unseen, if possible until they reached the priest's chosen destination. Sticking close to the wall in the direction they'd taken when leaving the tavern, he caught sight of the priest's black clerical attire at the tram stop, surrounded by other people. Beside him, Rozica, in her boyish outfit with her cap on, seemed to be listening to the priest's explanations. Now, from a distance, Dan could see the man more clearly: of average height, with a short, graying beard and a black felt hat. He wore a black wool coat over a long priest's cassock, which was also black. Though not young, there was something youthful in his reserved yet authoritative demeanor. This was evident, for he had managed to win Rozica's trust and imposed on Dan almost unyielding obedience. A tram arrived, and they boarded the front car. Dan leaped onto the steps of the rear car, quickly paying the conductor. Hidden behind a group of passengers near the front door, he kept his eyes on each face that exited at every stop. He wasn't sure how he would avoid being recognized by the priest, but this concerned him less than not knowing where Rozica was being taken. After quite a long route, the priest and Rozica got off at a stop, walking in the opposite direction of the tram. Dan disembarked behind other passengers, leaving some distance between himself and the priest. Across the street, a church bell tower rose in the distance, leading Dan to believe this was the priest's parish. Sheltering himself behind a tree at the edge of the street, he waited to see if they would head there. Once they crossed the street, the priest entered the church grounds. Dan continued to watch them and saw a building with a yellow-painted facade at the back of the courtyard, which seemed to be the rectory. The priest and Rozica went inside.

Satisfied that at least he now knew where he could find Rozica, Dan turned back toward the tram stop to return to the tavern where he was supposed to wait for the priest. Back in front of the train station, he hesitated about re-entering the restaurant, thick with the smell of tobacco and coal smoke from its corner heater. Outside, the sun glittered on piles of snow along the edge of the sidewalk, shining like diamonds. The softened cold of the night prompted Dan to linger on the streets until it was close to the priest's return time. He once again saw the church with its bell tower and decided to go in that direction. It was an ordinary morning, and he figured not many people would be there at this hour. Entering the church, he found only a few visitors gathered in front of an enormous stone-carved monument, a crucifix. Dan approached, making the sign of the cross. The crucifix before him was unlike anything he had ever seen. The cross, nearly the height of the vaulted ceiling, supported the nailed body of the suffering Lord Jesus Christ, with a crown of thorns around His head. The composition conveyed a chilling sense of deep suffering to those who gazed upon it through its powerful realism. Flanking the cross were two almost life size statues, completing the ensemble, representing the Virgin Mary and Saint John the Baptist. In front of him, a man reading from a tourist guidebook to the woman beside him let Dan understand that this crucifix had been carved from a single block of stone in 1417 by the German sculptor Peter Lantregen. The same sculptor had other works in churches in Brasov and throughout Transylvania. Dan lingered in the chapel a while, wondering where the priest intended to host him and how he would be able to maintain contact with Rozica.

# A Patriotic Duty

As the tram start moving along with Rozica and the priest, Ștefan Suțu, noticed a figure detaching from the side wall leaping onto the rear car door. Without seeing his face, he recognized the figure of the young man he'd left minutes earlier in the tavern.

"That nuisance is going to cause me trouble," Ștefan thought. "He's stubborn and difficult. I think I'll have to get rid of him."

He said nothing of this to Rozica, hiding his irritation caused by Dan, and tried to remain pleasant with the girl, who showed no interest in the sights passing before her, or the people around her, and even in him. To capture her interest, Ștefan began to share what he knew about the city's history:

"Do you know how old this city is? There are documents attesting to its existence as far back as the 12th century. At the Vatican, there are records signed by the Pope from that period. Originally, Sibiu was known as Hermann Stadt, meaning 'Herman's town,' though no one really knows who Herman was. Did you know we have houses that are over 600 years old? They're still in use. Sibiu was officially recognized as a city later, I believe, in 1366. In the 15th century, the Saxon University was established here, numerous guilds were formed, and it became the most important fortress in all of Transylvania. The fortress of Sibiu became so strong militarily that it withstood every Ottoman siege attempt in the 15th century. A century later, in 1599, Michael the Brave won the Battle of Şelimbăr, uniting for the first time Transylvania, Wallachia, and Moldavia as one country."

"Yes, but they killed him by beheading," Rozica said sadly.

"True. He was surrounded by many enemies. After the Turks were defeated by Austria in the 17th century, Transylvania became a principality of Austria, with its capital in Sibiu. In the 19th century, the Metropolitanate of Transylvania was established here, becoming the spiritual center from where Romanians expressed their ideas of national liberation. But now, it's time to get off; we've arrived."

After they got off the tram, Ştefan wanted to make sure Dan had also disembarked behind them, stopping just before crossing the road to check with a sideways glance if they were followed. Seeing Dan, his irritation toward this distrustful young man, who clung to him persistently, grew like rising dough. He felt spied upon by this mindless boy who stayed on his trail and could show up at his house unexpectedly or even at his church services.

"That mustn't happen," Ştefan told himself.

They entered the spacious church courtyard, where there was another building, the priest's residence. Skirting the main entrance of the house with its two steps in the front, they arrived at a smaller door on the side where the kitchen was located. Shyly, Rozica met inside an elderly woman bustling around a cooking stove. It was a large room with windows looking out into the yard on either side of the door through which they entered. In the center of the room was a large table covered with colorful oilcloth, surrounded by chairs. A tall, solid cupboard with two large doors stood against one wall, alongside a white enamel fridge and a shelf filled with pots of various sizes, completing the decor of the room, where several doors led to other spaces. Ștefan stopped to kiss the old woman's forehead, then introduced Rozica:

"Nana, this girl is going to stay with us for a few days…"

"What girl? I see a boy, plain as day!"

"She may look like a boy, but she's a girl! Her name is Rozica. She's in disguise," he said, laughing. "Understand? We need to turn her back into a girl. If she doesn't have any clothes, give her a skirt and one of my shirts to wear. Rozica, sit down; make yourself at home! Nana, do you have anything good to eat?"

"Well, there are eggs, cheese, butter, milk…"

"All right, Nana," he said.

"Rozica, listen, we've just come off the road. You don't know this, but in the train station, on the train, on the tram, there are many people who have lice. Some don't even know it. We must be cautious… I suggest you take off the clothes you traveled in and anything else you have in your pack and put them outside in the cold after you change into what Nana gives you. If you want, you can take a bath, but we need to light the boiler first. I'll do the same."

Obedient, Rozica rose from her chair. In the meantime, Nana brought out a dark pleated skirt and a men's white shirt.

"Where can I change?" asked Rozica.

Nana pointed to the bathroom and returned to the kitchen.

"Who is this girl?" she asked Ştefan.

"I met her on the train. Remember Simha, my former lover? This is her daughter."

"The Jewish woman? This is her daughter, and you've brought her here? Are you out of your mind?"

"No, Nana, don't take it that way. Just for a few days, she needs help. Her husband is imprisoned in Târgu-Mureş, and I promised to help her."

"And how exactly can you help her? Have you forgotten they almost threw you out of here because of your 'unhealthy' background? Remember all the doors you knocked on just so they'd leave you alone? And let me tell you something else: have you forgotten how much you suffered because of that Jewish woman who destroyed your future?"

"Oh, come on now… Simha had no part in it."

"Maybe, but she made you suffer… Didn't she? We all suffered because of it."

In the meantime, Rozica reappeared, transformed by the clothes she'd been given. Slender as a candle in a long skirt that reached her ankles, with the shirt tucked into the waistband and sleeves rolled up, she looked like a figure from an allegorical painting. Ștefan couldn't take his eyes off her face, so strikingly like that of his former lover from his youth. The stature, the features, the color and shape of her eyes, her lips, and even her short-cropped, golden hair, all were identical to Simha's. After more than two decades of torment, despair, and regret, Simha reappeared to him now, not as a mere apparition but real, vibrant with the same youth and vigor as the one who had left him. He stood up and moved, with the impulse to embrace her, but instead clasped her hands between his own.

"You are, how should I put it, a perfect copy of your mother. I've never seen such a striking resemblance. Looking at you, I know why I loved so much your mother…"

Rozica smiled, feeling overwhelmed and not knowing what to say. Nana placed the omelet on the plates set on the table alongside bread, butter, cheese, and glasses of milk. She didn't like at all what it was unfolding around her. This girl, Rozica, was going to drive mad again the man she took care of, since he was weaned from his mother. Knowing Ștefan's impulsive nature that had cost him so much in life, this girl he had brought into their home predicted unimaginable problems,. But what could she do, an old woman who had dedicated her life to a boy who never listened to anyone?

After eating, the priest brushed off his coat and shoes and, saying he had to go into town, left the kitchen.

"God bless you, Father," greeted a few elderly women coming to the church.

"The Lord be with you!" Ștefan replied, making the sign of the cross in their direction. He made way for them to enter the vestibule adorned with murals on walls shaded by rounded arches supported by stone columns that gave charm to this place of worship. On holidays and every Sunday, a few beggars would gather here, hoping for the alms of parishioners. Ștefan crossed himself as he approached the altar, then entered through the central door. After a few minutes of thought, he decided to look for Petrică Neacșu, the deacon who had been a longtime friend.

"What's new in the Capital?" Neacșu asked, shaking hands.

"Nothing much, building socialism. The Romanian News on television has just been launched."

"Don't say! How was it?"

"Impressive! Too bad the screens are so small."

"But tell me, did you hear what happened about students the protests at the University in Bucharest? I heard rumors that many students were jailed. They say the revolt was in protest over the Russians occupation of Hungary..."

"No, I hadn't heard."

"They even say they arrested Imre Nagy, Hungary's minister, here in Bucharest. Is it true?"

"What would I know? It might just be rumors. Better tell me what's new around here?" Ștefan asked.

"Not much. Had a little poker night at Prosecutor Bârsan's last night. Costed me about three poli (20 lei bills)."

"Who else was there?" Ștefan asked, curious.

"Colonel Matache from security and Ionescu from supply."

"I have an urgent message for Matache. Do you have someone trustworthy here who can deliver a note?"

"Where's the note?"

"I'll write it now."

He pulled a notebook from his coat pocket, tore out a page, and, taking out his fountain pen, scribbled a note, alerting Matache that a criminal named Daniel Cristescu, planning to flee abroad, is presently at the tavern near the train station. "I know he is pursued by security in Bucharest and waits for me to give him directions  to escape aboard. He's wearing a short black cloth coat and a black fur hat. Out of patriotic duty, I am informing you of what I know about this enemy of the state." He signed and folded the note and handed it to the deacon.

David Kimel

# The Trap

When Dan thought that it was time to return to the tavern, he looked once more at the crucifix in the chapel, crossed himself again, and stepped out onto the street. Rounding the corner towards the train station, he saw from a distance that a police car was parked in front of the tavern and stopped onto his tracks.

"What is the militia doing here?" Dan wondered. "Probably some patrons got into a fight, and someone called the police," he told himself.

He stayed where he was, waiting to see what would happen next. It wasn't long before two uniformed officers were dragging a man, nearly lifting him off the ground, as he struggled with them in protest. Dan squinted, trying to get a clearer look at the man being shoved towards the police car parked in front of the tavern. He was a man of about the same build as himself, wearing a short woolen coat and a black fur hat. A terrible suspicion clouded Dan's mind. Could the militia be looking for him? His resemblance to the arrested man was striking; they shared almost the same features. Even physically, they looked alike as the one taken by police was also a young person. Could the militia have received his photo from Bucharest and now be searching for him? No way! They had no way of knowing he was supposed to be at that tavern at this time. So, how did they end up there? Someone must have tipped them off. Who knew he was supposed to be there? Only the priest and Rozica!

"Then, the priest betrayed us!"

Dan immediately turned around and went back into the chapel. Now he had proof of the danger pursuing him. The militia had his information and the necessary description needed to arrest him. It would not be long before he'll be caught and thrown into a jail. He had to act quickly; there was no time to waste. But how?

For the moment, there in the chapel, on this sacred place he had the sanctuary needed. Surely, Dan thought, looking at the sorrowful figure of Christ on the cross, the Holy Spirit could inspire him as to what to do. He concentrated to figure out his first step, especially since now, he could be recognized not only by his figure, but also by his clothing. His short coat and fur hat were not much different from those of the man detained by the police.

"Lord, help me; you know better what I should do," Dan said, touching his forehead as he bowed in prayer.

Inside the chapel, a woman dressed in black, eyes fixed on the crucifix, seemed to be praying to the Lord in silence. She didn't look like a tourist but rather a local woman whose faith had led her to the foot of the cross. The same reason had brought him here, to this chapel where hope is resurrected. When he saw that the woman was about to leave, Dan stepped in front of her.

"Excuse me, are you from around here?"

"Yes. How can I help you?" she asked.

"Do you know if there's a free market anywhere today?"

"Now?"

"Yes, I need something I may find there."

"Well, there is the Big Market or the Small Market. I think you'll find what you need there."

"Is it far?"

"It's in the city center. One is in the upper town, and the other in the lower town, but they're close to each other."

"How do I get there?"

"Well, there might be a bus from here that goes there. But if you walk along the Main Street, you'll get there in about 10 minutes."

"Thank you. God bless you."

"Go with the Lord…"

After leaving the church, Dan asked around for directions to Main Street. When he reached the market, he saw a long row of stalls lined up in front of massive, old-style buildings. Food products, textiles, embroidery, sheepskin furs, lambskins clothes, and various household items were displayed for the crowd passing by. Dan met a man dressed in a dark-colored padded jacket introduced by Russian soldier's, and a fur hat with a red star on the forehead. At that time, many people had started wearing jackets like that wanted to show they are part of the proletarian class. Thinking that a jacket like that was exactly what he needs, Dan addressed him:

"Mister, can I ask you something?"

"What is it?"

"Look, if I give you my coat and hat, will you trade me your jacket and hat?"

"Why would I do that?" the man asked.

"Well, you see… I got a job at the railway as a stoker on a train. My coat is too tight for that work, and it would be a shame to ruin it, as it's brand new. How about a trade?"

The man hesitated, looked at Dan's coat from a distance, and said,

"Take it off so I can see if it fits."

Dan took off his coat and handed it to the man. He tried on the padded jacket himself. The man carefully examined Dan's things inside and out and accepted the trade. They parted with a handshake. With the military hat earflaps pulled down to cover the back of his neck and tied under his chin, Dan thought it would now be harder to be recognized. Seeing a mirror on one of the stalls, he looked at his face. With more confidence in his new appearance, he wandered a bit among the stalls and stopped in front of one selling valuable items like porcelain, silver cutlery, trays with sophisticated designs, dresses, silk shawls, and other items. Among them was a pair of wire-framed glasses. Dan stopped, picked up the glasses to try them on, and asked:

"Are these for sale?"

The man behind the stall, an elderly man with white hair and an absent expression, nodded.

"How much do they cost?"

"How much will you pay for them?"

"Five lei. Is that okay?"

"Okay."

With his disguise complete, Dan stopped, wondering what to do next. He couldn't stay in town for long. The train to Alba Iulia had left long ago, the train station was likely swarming with agents, and Rozica was in the greatest danger, held captive by the traitorous priest. If he tried to stay at a hotel, he'd have to show his ID. Even at a private residence, he'd have to be reported to the militia within 24 hours. Here in Sibiu, he knew no one, couldn't stay on the streets, and had nowhere to go. What was there to do? He saw a pastry shop across the street and went inside. He ordered a cream-filled savarin pastry and tea, then sat down at a table. Looking at his face in the oval mirror hanging on the wall, he found it hard to recognize himself. The glasses he wore made him feel dizzy but changed his appearance. In his mind, worry for Rozica, who was in danger, stirred plans of rescue that were hard to carry out. He didn't know how, but he had to reach her, tell her everything he knew about the priest, and get her out of his hands.

Protected by the padded jacket and the star-capped hat, he thought he might take the risk of a nighttime incursion into the church ground, though he didn't know if he'd be able to see Rozica. Dan lingered for a moment in the warm, pleasant pastry shop, then went out to wander on the streets. He walked randomly trying to memorize each location, the names of shops he passed, firms hanging above the windows and later came upon a tavern with a fixed menu.

After eating, Dan noticed a sign reading, "Albina Cultural Hall." He entered and found inside a theater hall where many young people were watching an amateur performance. He sat down on a chair and watched the stage absent-mindedly, his thoughts elsewhere. When the show ended, he thought it would be dark by now, and he should go to look for Rozica. He didn't know how, but it was essential to find her and warn her that the priest was an informer for the security forces. Dan planned mentally how he might sneak near the house behind the church in the dark, watch inside through the lit windows to see Rozica, and maybe he could even manage to get her out to speak with her.

When he went back out onto the street, Dan came upon the tram he had taken to the church. Following the tram tracks, he arrived in front of the church.

# Nana

After his conversation with Neacșu, Ștefan hurried home, knowing that Nana would be waiting for him as usual, with the table set and the food steaming in pots on the stove. Now, Rozica's presence irresistibly drew him in, just as her mother had once captivated him years before. There was no doubt that he was witnessing a miracle! If Rozica hadn't revealed that little, amber-handled pocketknife, he would never have discovered that she was Simha's daughter, and he wouldn't have felt the joy of rediscovering his former lover in her daughter. First and foremost, it was a miracle that the girl even sat next to him on the train. When he proposed that the girl stay with him, his intentions were sincere. He was truly moved by the plight of the young people he had met by chance on the train and felt, like any good Christian, that it was his duty to help them. But seeing the stubbornness of that young man, Daniel Cristescu, who could cause him endless trouble, Ștefan had to find a way to get rid of him. There was no other solution! Now, however, with the image of his former love revived, the question arose: what should he do with Rozica now that Dan's presence no longer mattered? Rozica could stay with him for a few days, with promises that he would bring her news from her husband, but how long could he keep her in this state? And then, what other excuses could he find to convince her to remain here? He would like to have Rozica by his side, to  introduce her as a visiting daughter of a cousin, perhaps even with the idea that she might settle there. But would Rozica accept such a situation? If not, then what could he do?

Obsessed with these thoughts, he entered the kitchen. As he had anticipated, the table was set with plates, cutlery, and even a decanter of wine placed on the tablecloth. Nana was still standing by the cooking stove, and Rozica, at the old woman's urging, was bringing the freshly baked bread and everything else needed to the table. When she saw Ștefan, Rozica paused, eagerly awaiting news about Dan, where he had been accommodated, and any updates about their plan. Ștefan carefully avoided her gaze and went into the bathroom. Sitting down at the table afterward, he mentioned that he hadn't found Dan at the tavern. He had asked the boys at the counter, but they told him that the young man had left the place a while ago.

"I think he decided to continue on his own," Ștefan said.

Rozica felt a pang of sadness at his words.

"No, Dan wouldn't do such a thing."

"Then I don't have any other explanation."

They ate in silence, served by Nana, who discreetly followed the conversation without asking what it was about. In Ștefan's absence, Rozica had confided in her, explaining that she had been with her friend on the train when she met the priest. Her friend was supposed to stay somewhere nearby. She had also mentioned that Ștefan had promised to bring her news from her husband, imprisoned in Târgu-Mureș, which was why she had come here with him. The girl's sincerity managed to slightly temper the old woman's hatred toward the young woman, the daughter of the one who had bewitched Ștefan, whom she had raised like a son. This girl might be sincere and perhaps even innocent, but once again, Ștefan seemed to be gripped by the same fever as in the past, and that was not a good sign.

After the meal, Ștefan retreated to his room to rest, as a sleepless night on the train and the day's events had left him utterly drained. He carefully placed his clothes on the back of a chair and lay down. With his eyes closed, he awaited the arrival of sleep, but it refused to come. He got out of bed to close the heavy brocade curtain, then lay down again. Now that he had managed to convince Rozica that Dan had left on his own, he continued to be troubled by the thought that, so far, Dan's arrest had not been confirmed. On the other hand, he feared that Dan might claim he wasn't alone, that he had been accompanied by Rozica on the train, though he knew Dan would gain nothing from that. But what if Ștefan wondered, the authorities hadn't found Dan where he had directed them? What if Dan had managed to evade his pursuers and was now wandering freely around the city? In that case, knowing where Rozica was, it wouldn't be surprising if he showed up at any moment in his own home... This could spark a major scandal that would cause him great harm. They would accuse him of harboring fugitives wanted by the authorities.

"God, what a mess I'm in…" With his conscience stirred by these thoughts, Ștefan realized he could no longer sleep. Fully awake, he went to the chair to put his clothes back on. He had to find out what had happened to Dan.

Returning to the kitchen, he found Nana and Rozica finishing up the cleaning. The dishes were in their place, and he had the impression that they were discussing something that he had interrupted. He mentioned that he had a little errand in town, leaving Rozica with the impression that he was going to investigate her situation, and stepped out onto the street. Across the road, on the wall of the grocery store, there was a public phone. He called Barsan, the prosecutor. Knowing him to be a decent man, Ștefan often got inside information from him.

"Hello, young man, how's the justice doing?"

"Oh, hello, Father. You're back from Bucharest?"

"Well, where could I feel better than in my own home?"

"Anything new in the capital?"

"Well, constructions everywhere. The transmission tower at

Casa Scânteii has been completed, with a huge television antenna at the top. I saw the first Romanian news broadcast on television! It's amazing to see that, my man! It seems, we're finally catching up with the world! But tell me, do you know Matache's phone number? I have some business with him…"

Barsan gave him the number, and Ștefan jotted it down in his notebook. After exchanging a few more polite words, he called Matache.

"How's the comrade colonel doing? Healthy and as strong as ever?" Ștefan asked on the phone.

"Hey, Father! We're doing well, same as always."

"Glad to hear it! So, did you catch that fellow from the train station?"

"They arrested one guy, but he had no connection. The one in your note hasn't been found…"

"Really?" the priest asked, startled.

"Yes, but don't worry! We'll catch him. We got now his photo circulated through Agerpres. (Romanian Agency of Press)"

"So, is he dangerous guy, right?"

"Seems so."

"Couldn't he's be heading to the Hungarian border? The counter-revolution isn't over there…" Ștefan suggested.

"Possible, but not by train. We checked. We're questioning the intercity drivers now. Don't worry, we'll catch him…"

Ştefan listened grimly to what Matache said. He sensed that his situation was worsening with each assurance from the officer. His legs, he felt, gone weak. He exchanged a few uninspired words with the colonel, then, hanging up the receiver, Ştefan walked worriedly back home. What could he tell the girl now that Dan could appear at any moment? Given the circumstances, he had to be on guard and alert to any movement or noise. Assuming Dan did show up, what would he do? Dan was younger, taller, and much stronger than him. If he came in violently and with ill intent, how would he be able to stop him, and with what would he defend himself?

Ştefan had no weapons in the house, not even a phone to call the police. He remembered that his request for a phone had gone unanswered for two years. Suddenly, he realized that his parish was completely isolated. There were streets on two sides, and no close neighbor around that could hear him if he ask for help. He had to arm himself! With this thought, he entered the church courtyard.

Before going inside, Ştefan went in the dark shed at the back of the yard, looking around for an ax and the pitchfork. He brought and leaned them outside against the kitchen door, trying not to alarm Nana or Rozica. He planned to bring these weapons inside the house later after they would go to sleep. Then he thought that, left there, Dan might use them to break into the house, so he laid them down beside the cellar entrance.

# Foam Always Gets the Top

After the priest left, Rozica collapsed onto a chair, resting her forehead in her hands as they leaned against the edge of the table. Nana watched her in silence, and seeing tears fall down the beautiful girl's face, she sat beside her and, avoiding to show pity, spoke with the natural wisdom of a simple woman.

"Girl, you don't belong here. I don't believe Stefan can help you with anything. He makes promises; it's his way, but he doesn't keep them. It's not that he doesn't want to; he just can't. He couldn't fool me; I raised him. So don't hesitate, just leave! Look, I'll bring your things to your room. Tonight, after he goes to sleep, leave here; there's nothing for you to wait for! Go with God wherever you think best. That's my advice."

Rozica looked at the grave, stone-carved face of the old woman and, taking her hand, leaned forward to kiss it, but Nana quickly pulled it away without a word. Only their eyes confirmed their understanding.

From Stefan's morose expression when he entered the kitchen, Nana and Rozica could tell something was wrong. They rose to prepare everything needed for dinner. For a while, a funeral-like silence filled the room. After hanging his coat on the hook behind the door, Stefan sat at the table where Nana brought the pitcher of wine and filled him a glass. After drinking it, he filled the glass again. Waiting for him to say something, Rozica asked:

"Did you find out anything about Dan's disappearance?"

Stefan shook his head in a way that suggested no.

"Is it possible that someone provoked him somehow, and he was taken to the police?"

Stefan, not in the mood to talk, responded with a dismissive wave.

"You're convinced he left me and went off on his own?"

"I don't know, girl. What am I, some fortune teller who knows everything?" the priest snapped at her.

"Oh, come on, Father. It won't kill you to answer a question," Nana interjected as she set the bowl of food on the table.

They ate in silence. After finishing, Stefan rose from his chair and told Rozica to rest because, in the morning, he planned to go with her to Târgu-Mureş, hoping she could visit her husband. At these words, Rozica froze, stunned by the priest's words. Could it be possible, after so much time without knowing if he was even alive, that she would finally see or get some news about her husband? It seemed unbelievable.

"What time do you want to leave?"

"Around five in the morning. With the first train, to give us as much time as possible…"

"Thank you, Father. May God bless you for your kindness!"

"I'm going to bed now. You should sleep too, so you're rested for tomorrow."

After the priest went into his bedroom, Nana saw Rozica's eyes sparkling with the joy of a possible miraculous reunion with her beloved husband the next day. Shaking her head in doubt, she pulled Rozica closer and whispered gravely:

"Don't listen to him, girl! I don't know what his plans are, but I don't believe he's truly going to help. Your only chance is to flee tonight, as we agreed."

"I can't, Mother," Rozica replied. "If there's even a one-in-a-million chance, I have to take it."

"It's your choice! Do what you think is best," the old woman said, leaving Rozica, who continued to savor the imagined moment of seeing her husband.

Soon, Father Stefan appeared at his bedroom door, dressed in a long nightshirt with peasant embroidery on the chest and slippers on his feet. He went straight to the kitchen cupboard, where he took out the large knife used for cutting the homemade bread that was as big as a wagon wheel.

"You're still not in bed?"

"No, but what are you planning to do with that knife?" asked Nana.

"I heard there are thieves about, and I have no other weapon if I need one," the priest replied. "Rozica, can I speak with you for a moment?"

"Yes, Father."

"Then come here. I want to explain something," he said, waiting for her by the door. "Sit here on the bed," he added, pulling up a chair in front of her. He placed the knife on the small nightstand next to the bed.

"We're going to Târgu-Mureş, but I haven't yet spoken to the person who could help us. I know how eager you are to see your husband or hear news about him. You want this resolved as quickly as possible, isn't that true?"

"Yes, it is."

"That's why I'm taking you with me tomorrow, so you can see for yourself that I'm doing everything for you. I'm doing this in memory of your mother, whom I loved deeply, though she betrayed me."

"She betrayed you?" Rozica asked, stunned by this confession. "How did she betray you?"

"I did everything for her; I wanted to marry her! My parents wouldn't accept her, saying they would disinherit me if I married her. That didn't matter to me, but she eventually married Mihai Cută, your father."

"Why did she do that? Didn't she love you?"

"Quite the opposite. She loved me madly. She left me because I'm a Christian…"

"I can't believe it. Not my mother! She was never religious."

"She wasn't, but your grandparents and the rest of your family were…"

Hearing Stefan's words, Rozica wrung her hands in the lap of the skirt Nana had given her.

"No, my mother didn't betray you! You yourself said she loved you madly. She suffered, perhaps as much as you did. I believe she sacrificed herself to bring you peace. I'm convinced it wasn't easy for her, but she wanted reconciliation with everyone, with you, with your family, and with hers. That's not betrayal; it's an act of heroic courage!"

"What kind of heroic act do you see in that? She ruined my life! Why do you think I donned the priest's robe? For pleasure?... Because of her, I have no family, no children, nothing. She, however, had all that. So, who sacrificed more, her or me? Why don't you speak of my heroic act? Why don't you answer?"

Rozica didn't know how to respond. In a way, it seemed he was right too. The tension of this discussion, which she found herself unwillingly involved in, exhausted her. It was a story from the past, where nothing could be changed, least of all by her. She wanted to stand up and leave, but Stefan became impatient. His chin trembled in anger as he struggled to find the right words quickly, perhaps also affected by the wine he had drunk at dinner.

"Can I go to bed now?" she asked.

"No, stay a bit longer. You don't understand. I loved her so much. No one did for her what I did. Do you think she would have enjoyed the career she had without my help? I introduced her to the most aristocratic families, to the company of the most talented artists of the time, and even to the palace. Did she ever tell you that the king danced with her and asked to meet her?"

"No. Who? King Michael?"

"No, his father, King Carol II."

"I didn't know."

"Yes. She was a great success. She was admired by everyone… But when I became a monk because of her, she never came to the monastery to see me. When I wrote to her, she didn't answer my letters. That was the reward for everything I did for her.

See? That's betrayal!"

"What can I do now?"

"You? Do you still ask? You're not yourself; you are her risen from the dead! I'm speaking to her right now! God brought you to me to repay my suffering," Stefan said, sitting beside her on the bed.

Rozica tried to get up, but he pulled her back, holding her by the shoulders.

"Don't you understand? You are Simha, the one I loved my whole life… I lost her once; I can't lose her again. You must stay here with me forever!"

Rozica looked at him with frightened eyes, not understanding anything. This man was no longer the priest she had spoken with the previous night on the train; beside her now was a madman, filled with rage, his eyes glassy, his behavior out of control. He pulled her shoulders toward his chest, covered in the nightshirt's fabric.

"You are my love, my only love, reborn. I can't live without you," Stefan continued, inflamed as he gripped her tightly in his arms. Rozica struggled to break free from his hold, but he bent his mouth over her neck, attempting to kiss her.

"No, Father, come to your senses! You are a man of the

church; the Lord will punish you if you sin," Rozica yelled, seeing she couldn't escape him.

"The Lord sent you to me! He gave you to me as a reward for my years of suffering. You are mine now," Stefan continued, bending heavily over her, pinning her across the bed. Rozica fought with him, trying to free herself, but he pressed his knee over her thighs, trapping her. She managed to push her foot against the bed's headboard.

"Don't resist. I love you as I loved her. You are mine now," Stefan said, sliding a hand into her shirt neckline while using his other hand to pull her skirt up, exposing her thighs.

"Nana, help!" Rozica screamed with all her might. "Nana!... Nana, help me! I think the priest has gone mad… Help!"

He continued to hold her firmly, pressing his body into the space between her legs. As she writhed beneath him, screaming, he tried to kiss her on the mouth. But he couldn't, as Rozica twisted, getting her head close to the high headboard of Stefan's bed. Here, she spotted the knife brought from the kitchen and grabbed it by the handle. Turning her head to avoid his mouth, Rozica thrust the knife's sharp point into his shoulder until she felt it hit something hard. She pulled the knife out and struck again.

In agony, Stefan stood up, howling, stumbled over the chair he had sat in moments before, and managed to reach the door. Just then, Nana appeared to see what was happening. Seeing Stefan's blood spattered on his beautiful nightshirt, and Rozica raised on the bed, her chest and thighs exposed, still holding the knife threateningly in her hand, the old woman was horrified. Stefan felt his wounds, and when he saw his hand covered in blood, he collapsed unconscious on the thick carpeted floor.

"You wretch, you killed my son! You killed my son! What am I going to do?" Stunned, she quickly left the room.

"Help, my son has been killed!" she shouted as she opened the door to the yard.

"Help! Someone, please!"

Stepping out into the yard, she encountered a man in the dark, wearing a Russian winter coat and a cap with a red star on his forehead. Pointing to the open door, she said:

"In the house. My son has been killed!" Then she ran into the street.

"Help! Help, my son has been killed! People, my son has been killed…"

The old woman's cries roused a few neighborhood dogs, who joined her with sleepy barks. A few windows lit up in the middle of the night, and two people appeared at their gates along the street.

The man in the Russian coat cautiously entered and, reaching Stefan's bedroom door open, saw Rozica frozen near the disheveled bed, her chest bare, holding a knife in her hand. Not far from her feet lay a man face down, his nightshirt soaked in blood. The stranger bent over the body on the floor to see if he was still alive. Seeing this man in the Russian coat so close to her, half-undressed and fearing another attacker, Rozica gripped the knife with both hands over her head and plunged it into the newcomer's back before he could stand up. The man in the winter coat collapsed over the priest's body.

After a moment of hesitation, when she saw the stranger was no longer moving, Rozica leaned over him. When she turned his face toward her, she pulled back in terror, covering her eyes with her hands. It was Dan. With his glasses falling from his nose, his face pale, and his eyes closed, he was still breathing. She saw his brow furrowed in discomfort from the glare of the ceiling light, then opening his eyes slowly recognizing her, delivered a murmuring sound:

"Rozica..."

# The Return of the Prodigal Sons

At the old woman's cries, a few neighbors gathered to see what had happened. Entering the house, they found a girl on her knees, bending over one of the victims, cradling his head in her lap. Another victim, dressed in a nightshirt, was groaning nearby. Around the victims, on the floor, there was a pool of blood and a knife with blood stains. Someone ran to the public phone at the grocery store to call for an ambulance and police. No one dared to enter the room with the victims until the ambulance arrived. The groaning figure on the carpet was immediately recognized: it was Father Ştefan Suţu from the local parish. The ambulance attendants carried him from the room on a stretcher, and as he regained consciousness, he struggled to remember what had happened. Beside him, walking alongside the stretcher, Nana, with disheveled hair and a tear-streaked face, held his hands, lamenting:

"The Jewess killed my son! Yes, she killed my son…"

When the police arrived, they pulled the girl from the room, and an officer began questioning her. Meanwhile, the second victim, still alive, was taken out on a stretcher in the second ambulance, which had arrived soon after the first. To identify the victim, they asked the girl:

"What's the victim's name?"

"Daniel Cristescu."

"Address?"

"He doesn't have one. He's from Bucharest," the girl replied, her eyes red but her face stoic, ready to face whatever challenges lay ahead. She stood before the officer, upright, composed, and waiting for his questions:

"Who attacked the victims?"

"I did."

"Why?"

"To defend myself."

"To defend yourself from the father?"

"Yes."

"Why?"

"He tried to rape me."

"How? What do you mean?"

"Sexually."

"That's not possible. I don't believe you! I think you are lying! And the second victim?"

"I didn't know who he was."

"Now you know?"

"Yes, he's, my partner."

"Why did you try to kill him?"

"I was afraid. I didn't know who he was, dressed in that thick coat…"

"How did you end up in the priest's house?"

"He brought me here."

"Why?"

"He said he wanted to help me."

"In what way?"

"He promised to help me find news about my husband, who's imprisoned in Târgu-Mureş jail."

"Did he?"

"No. He tricked me. His real intention was to take advantage of me."

Unconvinced, the officer decided to handcuff the woman and tasked her to the station. There, they would find out the real motive behind the woman's attempt to kill two people.

At the hospital, it was determined that Father Ştefan Suţu's wounds were not serious, so he would be allowed to return home and resume his duties within a few days. However, as the young woman's accusations of attempted rape were substantiated by her investigators, the Church decided to defrock him following a six-month prison sentence.

As for Daniel Cristescu, the chest wound had caused lung injuries, requiring extended medical care. During his fight for his life, between days of high fever and sub-conscientious dreams, Dan tried to remember what happened, reconstructing from memory his actions of that day. He saw himself waiting from the darkened street by the church fence for a chance to speak to Rozica. At the back of the priest's house, a couple of rooms were illuminated, and looking around the street to see if there were people watching him, Dan decided to get closer. As he approached the illuminated area, Dan heard a woman screaming from inside. As he got near, the back door suddenly opened and a woman rushed out calling for help:

"Help! Someone, help, please! In the house", said the woman, pointing to the door as she saw Dan nearby:

"My son was killed!" Then, the old woman ran into the street, continuing to cry for help.

When he stepped inside, Dan remembered seeing Rozica in the middle of that horrifying scene with a knife in her hand and a man lying at her feet. Then everything became blurry; he could remember he bent down to see if the victim on the floor was still alive, but then something happened that caused him to fall, too. That's the thing he cannot explain: What happened there? Why is he here, lying on a bed surrounded by nurses? And why does he feel such an acute pain in the back, below his shoulder? He could not forget that Rozica was crying, holding his head on her lap, and after that, everything lapsed, and he could not remember anything. The doctors said that he was stabbed with a sharp object. A sharp object? Rozica had a knife in her hand. Could she have stabbed him? But why? No, that could not be possible, he told himself. Why would she want to kill him? There was no reason to believe such a thing. But if that did happen, perhaps she was scared, and she tried to defend herself. Maybe in despair, she thought he was someone else wearing that ugly coat and a red star-holding cap he exchanged in the market.

Regaining his conscience, Dan realized that he was supervised not only by the medical staff but also by a police officer sitting by the door.

"Am I under arrest?" he asked.

"Your case is under review," the policeman answered.

"What happened to the woman who was there with me?"

"She's being investigated at the station."

Before his release from the hospital, Dan was interrogated

by some officials about his intentions to flee the country and his reasons for doing so. Upon reviewing their files at the police station, authorities were looking for both suspects as they were already under surveillance by security in Bucharest, and they were sent separately there for further investigation.

After months of inquiries into the charges, Dan remained in detention leading up to his trial. He was never permitted to see Rozica while being told that she confessed to their true intentions and the crimes they committed together. Finding out that his trial was to start soon, Daniel wanted to have comrade Bărbulescu, with whom he worked at the Metallurgical Plant, defend him. His request was denied on the grounds that comrade Bărbulescu never had a case disputed as a lawyer in an instance. During their trials, neither Dan nor Rozica were permitted to have close relatives, friends, or witnesses in attendance. They had no one who could speak in favor to their character or bring some important information about their past life. The defendants assigned to them were barely provided a chance to explain what had happened that led to their real cause of action.

After Dan and Rozica were found guilty of their crimes, they were brought in front of their co-workers from the technical services at the Metallurgical Plant, where they were finally could see each other after that horrific night in Sibiu. Their old work colleagues were gathered in the same meeting room where Dan used to work, in which comrades Roşca, the Party Secretary, comrade Budău, the Chief Engineer, and a Security officer informed them about the numerous crimes they committed against the working class. However, the people's vigilance under the leadership of their Communist Party stopped their actions before they happened, and now they were brought there to face the anger of their own comrades who would not tolerate such behavior. While many in the audience watched the saddened faces of the inmates boxed by policemen in front of the presidential table, trying to associate what they heard with their own knowledge of these people, some started accusing them for their criminal actions, condemning Dan inexcusable love affair with an adulterous woman who influenced an infatuated the young man to steal money from his working comrades. Rozica and Dan were accused of inveterate hate against the working-class people, as it was proven without doubt by her intention to flee the country to the enemy line, and she successfully manipulated Dan Cristescu to leave with her. That is an inexcusable act of treason which must be applied to both. The loudest voices at the meeting were those of comrades Rosner, Mănoiu, engineer Istrate, and Nestorescu, who had to pay back all the people who were defrauded.

Following this meeting, Dan and Rozica were once again separated and brought back to their cells at different locations around the country. Nothing was ever heard again of David Şfarţ, Rozica's husband. She was incarcerated in a women prison and were escorted daily under heavy security to work at different construction sites or at some agricultural fields. The physical work was hard, but it didn't exhaust her as much as her constant fear that she'd not be able to survive her ten-year sentence.

Dan was also sent to various construction sites for hard labor until he was moved to the Danube-Black Sea Canal construction site soon after it opened. There, his eight-year conviction allowed him to see unimaginable horrors and abuse acts applied to people forced to execute orders by their jailers. Like him, Rozica also suffered during her imprisonment, the deplorable conditions she and others were forced to endure, the hard work and the cruelty prisoners faced under abusive guards that caused some inmate's deaths. They would never be able to forget these years and days, all the injuries, pain and scars inflicted so deep in their conscience that cannot be described.

Yet after many years, Dan and Rozica were finally permitted to correspond by mail, receiving heavily censored letters that brought a slim glimmer of hope into their bleak existence. A ray of optimism grew in their hearts as they read and re-read between lines words of sorrow, hope and love, leaving each of them to look and feel the possibility of better days after they would regain liberty. Their love, a sweetless love, that led them to the infernal life of detention trying to find happiness in Holly Land, may shine sometime in the future as a real, peaceful life.

# **About The Author**

Born in Bucharest, Romania, in January 1934, David Kimel witnessed the changes and turmoil of his country, dragged by forces beyond its control in the era preceding, during, and after the Second World War. Raised on the periphery of the city, surrounded by poor to middle-class neighbors, he learned at an early age the existence of prejudice, the lessons of survival which kept his Jewish family afloat through tough times, and gave him the strength to grow as a man.

After finishing an industrial school, he was selected by the Romanian Writers Union in 1952 for a scholarship at "Şcoala de Literatură şi Critică Literară Mihail Eminescu," an eminent literary academy for young writers, where he had the opportunity to meet the most prominent writers as teachers and colleagues. But he couldn't satisfy the regime's requirements and found work in industry. He married, had children, and immigrated to Canada in 1975, after a waiting period of eight months for a visa in a Greece refugee camp.

In his new country, he finally got a designer job with Magna International, a multinational company for automotive parts, where he held a leading position until retirement. He started to write again when his children became young adults. Among the many publications where he began collaborating, *Observatorul* (The Observer), a Romanian magazine in Toronto, created a permanent column, "Subjective," where his articles have appeared regularly for almost 20 years.

Many books in English and Romanian featuring his name have been printed since 2008. Among them, *Simple Seeds*, a poetry book printed by Author House, and *A Foggy Sunrise*, published by iUniverse. Two books, *A Sweetless Love* and *In the Pursuit of Happiness*, are presently in the process of printing.

In Romanian, David Kimel brought to light the novels: *Domniţa şi Tudor Avădanei* and *Capcana*; the short story collections *În Căutarea Fericirii* and *Anişoara*; a book of poems *Flori de Toamnă*; a memoir *Zori Înceţoşate*; a travelogue through many countries, *Din Lumea Largă*; and a collection of published articles, *Disecarea Timpului Prezent*, printed in Romania.

David Kimel is a member of the Romanian Writers Association of Canada (ASRC), the Writers and Editors Network, and the recipient of a Second Prize in the International Competition of Saga Printing House for the short story titled *Domnul Bratu*.